The Noble Stallion

NOBLE STALLION

by

Arthur-Heinz Lehmann

Translated from the German by
JAMES AND MARIKA CLEUGH
Illustrated by B. Biro

Henry Holt and Company «» *New York*

C. 2

BL

The Story

*T*he tale is told by a fellow crazy about horses, straight from the heart and just as his thoughts run off the pen. His heart is shared by a horse and a woman. It is big enough to love them both. The man is a simple sort of chap. But he has no nonsense about him. He is just the kind that women like and good horses are glad to have in the saddle. He is going to relate, in the brisk and cheerful spirit of a born rider, the adventures, pleasant or unpleasant, just as they occurred, of a horse and two people.

But he didn't altogether trust himself to write this book quite alone. He intended all along, as soon as he had put over the job on his own, to get someone to give it a thorough revision, in case he had expressed himself, here and there, in too crudely masculine a fashion. The punctuation, too, he thought, had better be put in afterward. He didn't want to be bothered with that, for he's more at home in the saddle than crouching over a desk.

So he asked a friend to provide the necessary bridling and control of the Pegasus in question. This friend did his very best to ride the mettlesome steed on a loose and easy rein, without pressing a single word into the service of "literature." The idea was to keep the free and natural style that is no less important in writing than it is in riding.

The Noble Stallion

THE NOBLE STALLION, referred to in the book as "The Majestic One," is a horse of outstanding beauty and character and as such attracts the attention of two delightful and rather Bohemian people—an ex-cavalry officer and a young Hungarian Countess. Most of the story takes place in a small village near Salzburg, but it goes back a few years to a district in Western Styria where famous horses are raised.

The Countess has come to look for a horse to add to her stable, and the ex-officer is there because of his love of horses. The two not only find their ideal horse, but they fall in love with each other. Their enthusiastic devotion to horses catapults them into a series of hilarious and risqué adventures that provide entertainment of the first order. The amusing characters who participate in their adventures add color and interest to what is already a lively and sparkling story.

1

The sun it was, ye glittering gods,
ye took to make a horse!

—Dirghatamas

*I*t's a bad rider who never praises his horse.

I want to tell you about the loveliest and finest horse that ever lived. It's mine, too. You've got to believe that. I also want to tell you about the loveliest and finest woman that ever lived. As for her being mine, well, I should like to believe so, anyhow.

Then there's myself, the man she, the woman, calls "Unholy George." With us three you'll have the ground-work of the picture in place.

First we'll take a look at the stallion. He comes of ancient and noble stock. The only possible names he could have would be, as custom demands, those he inherited from his father and mother. They are Maestoso and Austria.

You'll only be giving him his due if you simply call him the "Majestic One," as we ourselves do.

His color is the most dazzling white you ever saw in your life. He's the proudest and fieriest stallion that mares ever whinnied after. He's the steadiest goer that ever put such power and grace at the service of a rider . . .

Next morning, when I looked through what I had written the night before, on this first page, I wanted to cut the lot. Those three dots at the end didn't mean I intended to stop writing. But I had to break off prematurely. At that very moment the Majestic One neighed in his stable. The sound struck my ears with the shrillness of a fanfare of trumpets. The vet happened to be driving by at the time, on his way to a calving cow. The scent of his three-year-old mare had been wafted to the Majestic One's nostrils through the open door of his stable. That mare was a darling, too. It was a shame she had to draw that rickety cart for the benefit of a vet who had once been chucked out of the inn for winning so much at tarok that even the priest, who's shortsighted and consequently takes a rosy view of everything, suspected there was something wrong. That little mare would have made the right sort of sweetheart for the Majestic One. He said so whenever he caught a whiff of her. I sympathized with him. For I consider myself no better than he is. And I know how it feels when you fall in love like that and never get any further, in spite of all the blood in your body running to your heart. Well, so the Majestic One's call rang out till it blared like all the trumpets of Jericho. But a poor devil of a man may be at the right age, just like his stallion, and yet he can't send out a neigh like that. Possibly he just sits down and writes a nice letter, hinting in all sorts of ways at what's worrying him. The woman who gets the letter, though, hears the silent paper neighing like one o'clock. Some very surprising things do happen, to be sure, during a declaration of love. Other things also happen, at the same time, that don't surprise anybody. But in the end the whole thing really is a surprising affair.

Well, anyhow, the Majestic One trumpeted so heart-rendingly that I jumped up from my desk and dashed out to his stable to console him. Two unhappy creatures are always the best at exchanging consolations. For in such a case compassion is mutual and quite genuine. The Majestic One's trouble about that little mare of the vet's resembled my own about my Hungarian girl friend. She had just left me again, as she had been doing for years, to join her horses, which were grazing on the Puszta. The Majestic One's a good deal better off than I am. He keeps faith with me all right. But he's bighearted where mares are concerned. One of them has only to put her hoofs down daintily, another one has only to poise her head gracefully on its slender neck, a third has only to carry her tail with a certain charm. And if they all have such a wonderful perfume that his nostrils quiver when he neighs, as if he were half seas over, well, then he makes no secret of his passion. He sends out a call to each and all of them. And he's not just making inquiries with it, but giving an order. The Majestic

One, if he had his own way, would be a regular sultan. All the same, he really loves only one mare, Deflorata. She belongs to his own noble Lipizza stock. But she is far away on the Puszta, at the very spot where my own Hungarian girl friend is also living. Personally, I don't behave like the Majestic One. I have a hard time of it. But a man must know how to control himself. It seldom looks well when one woman catches him out at his pranks with another.

Well, I was just crossing the yard, in the dark, when I tripped over something soft, my feet went flying, and I sat down with a bump. It wasn't a very hard one, for I had collapsed in a heap of the Majestic One's droppings. All the same, I found I couldn't get up again. Something had gone pop in my left ankle.

I started cursing and swearing at the Majestic One. He might have the decency, I told him, not to put such stumbling blocks in one's way when one's dashing to his rescue with a heart overflowing with affection. It's not a nice feeling, I added, when one comes crashing out of the skies of ardent love into a lot of horse dumplings. But my painful emotions were soon canceled out by the pain in my ankle. The latter actually afforded me some relief from my sorrow for the time being.

But as soon as I had managed to blunder to my feet and stagger into the house I would willingly have taken ten wounded hearts in exchange for that cockeyed ankle of mine.

The whole foot had swollen up inside the boot and merely to touch the leather made me feel as though I were atoning for all the past and future sins of my entire existence.

Well, I got through the night somehow and at five o'clock

4 ～

the next morning, when I heard the vet coming back from his calf delivery, driving his flirt of a mare that had been the cause of all the trouble, I called him in to put my sick foot to rights. He had to unpick the seam from the leg of my boot. The ankle had come up as thick as a dray horse's knee.

He gave the swelling a good bit of massage. Then he said, "Leg's all to hell, old boy."

"Broken?" I asked.

He nodded, adding that there had also been a fine old hemorrhage and possibly strained sinews as well. He spoke exactly as if he had been examining a lamed farm horse.

It occurred to me, however, that a vet might not be such an expert on the human leg after all and that it might not be half so bad as he said. He put a bandage round the ankle and told me he would look in two, three or four days later, when he paid another visit to the calf, which he had had to haul into this world at a rope's end. I should have to take a good long rest, he said, and keep that ankle quiet, to give it time to heal.

He had no sooner finished speaking than a hell of a row started outside. The Majestic One must have been kicking the hatch of his summer loose-box and the bolt, which had been pretty useless for some time, must have given way. Anyhow, when we looked to see what was going on out-of-doors, the Majestic One, large as life, was in the thick of it with the vet's mare, the shafts of the cart cracking and splintering. The mare didn't show the slightest sign of alarm but was doing all she could and tugging away at the harness to make things easier for the Majestic One.

"Damn you! You blasted he-goat!" yelled the cattle doctor, meaning the Majestic One. He dashed out of the house in a panic, thinking his cart was going to be kicked to bits. I joined in his curses, for all I was worth, from the window, quite forgetting my ankle.

"What do you want to drive her for when she's in heat, upsetting my stallion like that? He's got his feelings just like a man!"

"Yes, just like his owner, who's well known all round here for that sort of thing!" retorted the cattle medico, going for the Majestic One with his whip. The stallion reared, as he had been taught in the Riding School, and defended himself by slashing at the vet with his forefeet.

I backed the Majestic One up, yelling at the cattle doc: "Just you touch him once, you pig doctor, and you'll get every flower pot in the place at your head!"

But I didn't have to bombard him with the Hungarian's flower pots after all. I only tipped one of them over in one of my frantic gestures. The vet—after telling me he wasn't going to forget I had called him a pig doctor—retreated in very bad order to the driving seat, gave the mare a terrific walloping, and off the two of them dashed, hell for leather. The Majestic One snorted a few times and shook his head, till his snow-white mane sparkled in the sunshine. Then he went back into his box, shoulders and neck sagging, for I'd sent a bellow of disgust after him, which meant that he ought to be ashamed of himself.

Well, the cattle doctor naturally wouldn't look in on me again after that, since he now had it in for us both. Consequently, the idea of rest was out, for the two of us, after all, would have to eat. All the same, that tempest did do a bit of good. Punishment for once fitted the crime in this case, which was that of the mare. She had teased the Majestic One till he had lost all control of himself and that was just what she wanted. So she got a whacking and that was only fair, of course. But in my opinion it was quite unnecessary. A horse doctor like that doesn't understand the psychology of a lovesick mare. He cold-bloodedly puts it all down to purely physiological causes and then when his shafts get splintered he does nothing but curse. He thinks love in the case of a horse no good for anything but breeding. But horses aren't sows, or bunny rabbits either. They have a fine combination of human qualities, such as any of ourselves might well envy. As soon as the Majestic One showed, round about his seventh year, that the fillies were beginning to make an impression on him, I started treating him just like a man. It doesn't suit a proud stallion to live like a monk. I remember a poor horse, a stallion, which was always being ridden, forequarters gripped and hindquarters beaten. Whenever he made a bound, because he didn't know what else to do with his energy, he was punished. Well, every time that happened his master and rider fell off. So the master tried to crush the poor brute's spirit by using spurs and whip and half starving him of his oats. It got to such a pitch at last that the horse turned sullen. The heat of his blood affected his brain and it was all up with him. Don't tell me horse sacrifice is a thing of the past. Our ancestors at least had a reason for what they did in this line. But today the way we do horses in is sheer folly. It would be far better to make a stallion a hack right away by reducing him to the rank of gelding.

Well, I don't care what the horse doctors may say, the

Majestic One's gay life has done him a lot of good. It's true that the priest once called him the most immoral horse in the whole country. But it's all very fine for him to talk. He's forbidden to sin by his cloth. And anyhow his age stops him breaking out. And he doesn't have to ride the stallion either. Moreover, it's not his business to worry about colts or have heart-to-heart talks with mares.

As a matter of fact, this last May another foal did turn up in the village. The Majestic One must have jumped the hedge into the next field. A half-bred English mare had been whinnying there for such a time that at last he took pity on her. If the foal grows up as well as it promises to, we shall find that Lipizzaners and English half-breds produce quite decent horses.

To clinch the matter, the cattle doctor's mare is from Kladrub and a distant cousin of the Majestic One, so it's all quite understandable. You may be wondering why I should still be so full of the Majestic One's praises when my broken ankle was really all his fault. Well, I love him. And if he were ever to give me a kick by sheer accident, I should simply take a look at his hoof to see if it had got damaged at all in the process. You can call me crazy about horses if you like. But I only wish I could make plenty of others follow my example. Horses would then have a better time of it in this world.

Well, as soon as the cattle medico and his mare had rattled away and the Majestic One had slunk back into his box, my ankle started going for me in a big way and kept me on my back for quite a time. There could be no question of even thinking of feeding or grooming. I actually forgot, myself, that I was hungry.

After a while I heard the Majestic One snorting outside. He looked in at the window and I could see real hunger wrinkles at the corners of his mouth. I told him to take himself off to the paddock, only a hundred yards away. But apparently he didn't feel like eating grass. He started on the rock garden. He ate up the edelweiss and the gentian. I got a severe lecture about that later on when the Hungarian turned up and found her rock garden gone. But as she didn't arrive for some time that episode doesn't really fit in here at the moment.

The priest looked in during the morning. His hair is just as white as my horse's. But it's not so fine and silky. It's got more horsehair in it.

"If you're not an expert on smashed ankles, Father," I told him, "I don't need you. My *soul* is all right!"

"Ay, ay, Unholy George," he rejoined mildly. "You're a man of regular habits, aren't you? It's a sin a day with you, I know. Whose bedroom window have you been falling out of now?"

It's hard to bear when people label you for the rest of your life. I really believe that if I were to found a home for fallen girls out of my own pocket, the priest would be sure that all I should be thinking of afterward would be keeping the house full up. I told the spiritual shepherd, pretty sharply, that it was a shameful thing to make an invalid feel worse by bringing false charges against him instead of offering him consolation. After that, the priest shook out some oats for the Majestic One and promised to send someone over to look after me.

The next thing was that a person turned up whom I

9

should certainly have ordered to leave at once if she hadn't come out of neighborly affection.

It was Lois' girl friend, Mirl, and there was a very good reason why I wished she had stayed away. Lois is a friend of mine and is no more a peasant than I am. But we are tolerated in the village because we don't make ourselves conspicuous and the farmers sympathize to some extent with the way we spend our time. As I expect you have all noticed by this time, I'm by no means a pedant about my riding or, unfortunately, nowadays, about my writing either. I just indulge in either whenever I feel like it. As for Lois, he paints and carves and models in the same way. What I have in my brainpan, he has in his fists. Mirl's his great stand-by. She prepares his food, makes his bed, and types his letters. For he's always having rows with the city art dealers, who will never pay as much as he wants them to. So Mirl is a kind of handy woman. But she's not an old hand. She's only just over twenty and such a good all-rounder that Lois always tells the priest, whenever the latter asks, as he does every week, when he may put up the banns: "Oh, Mirl! Why *marry* her!"

Old Lois still wants to keep his freedom. But he's tied up tight just the same. He's in no better case, in that respect, than I am with my Hungarian. Still, man is a creature of illusions and it will be long before he's ever anything else.

Our priest, incidentally, calculates quite shrewdly. He is pretty sure that if ever anything happened to Mirl which produced a household of three, there would be a marriage in double quick time. For this reason he gives those two the advice to remain lovers, so long as they don't make it too obvious to the peasants, the point being that this is a special case in which he encourages a relationship his profession would otherwise oblige him to condemn.

I'd like to know, all the same, whether our priest really believes everything he preaches from the pulpit, as well as on less formal occasions. The fact that our consciences in this village remain so elastic simply proves how hard we try to live a respectable life. The trouble is, we can't always manage it.

Well, Mirl, you know, makes me sympathize with the Majestic One's weakness for the cattle doctor's mare. But as my friendship with Lois is more important to me than being sinful with Mirl, I keep out of her way whenever I meet her alone. It's a very critical period at the moment, as Lois is in Vienna and poor Mirl is left behind, quite defenseless. And the priest, in his simplicity, goes and sends her to *me!* It's temptation itself. I don't know whether his idea is to put me on the spot, since I'm quite helpless with my ankle out of action, or whether in this case his understanding of human feelings, of which he might ordinarily be more proud than of his theological learning, has let him down.

Mirl wanted to start on my bandage right away. She has had lots of experience with snapped ankle bones, Lois being much more enthusiastic about skiing than skillful at it. She told me, too, that the cattle medico knew nothing whatever about human anatomy, while she herself had had an excellent grounding in the subject from Lois, whose statues are always structurally accurate down to the last physical detail.

But I told her she'd much better fry me some bacon and eggs, as otherwise I should probably collapse there and then, on the sofa, from starvation.

She did so. And while I was eating she kept her bright blue eyes, a queer feature in that pale face of hers, framed in coal-black hair, fixed unwaveringly upon me. Those eyes, at such short range, embarrassed me so much that she asked: "What's the matter? Is there anything else you want?"

I couldn't very well tell her what I most wanted. She could easily have answered that I ought to be ashamed of myself for thinking of that sort of thing with a game leg on me. She may or may not have remembered Lois. I really couldn't say. A man can't think of so many things at once when there's one that's turning his whole head upside down.

As soon as Mirl, to my great relief, had taken her departure, I determined to let the Hungarian know what a mess I was in. She'd be sure to come, then, at top speed. That is, if she were really serious about the affair which had now been going on between us for the Majestic One's whole lifetime. But I couldn't write and tell her that I had simply tripped over a lot of horse dung. I should have to say that the injury had been caused in much more heroic fashion. Otherwise she would merely smile sympathetically, whereas I wanted her to be surprised to find me still alive. Well, I could easily fake a plausible story. It was only we two who could ride the Majestic One. He obeys me because he knows he can't do anything against me. And he goes like a lamb when the Hungarian's up, for he loves her and would hate to do her any harm. I'd like to find out some time what there really is between those two. But I shall never get to the bottom of it. Even the relation between the Hungarian and myself is a mystery to me.

I'd better not write, either, I reflected, about her having to replant the rockery, or about Mirl having been to see me. Really, there would be no sense in writing at all. Three days would have to go by and meanwhile anything might happen here, where I was in the thick of all sorts of dangers. The best thing would be to send a wire. But it could only go from Salzburg. I wasn't going to give the village postmaster the chance to start gossiping about the lies I should have to tell the Hungarian about my leg. And I couldn't telephone either, because the only phone in the place belongs to the postmaster. I couldn't send anyone to Salzburg because the only person I could rely on in a bit of sharp practice like this was Lois. And he was in Vienna. So I should have to go to Salzburg myself. But merely to think of harnessing the Majestic One to the dog-cart, the springs of which are as hard as iron and send the flesh rocketing off one's bones, put me right off the idea. The only alternative would be to saddle the Majestic One and ride him quietly, at a walk, or a gentle snail's gallop, to the post office at Salzburg, and send off the wire there. It would then only be read by the local official, who would have to hold his tongue on account of being professionally sworn to secrecy. If we started now, at a nice, slow pace, taking two hours there and two hours back, we could be in Salzburg by coffee time and home again for supper.

Well, I don't have to tell you what torture it is to hop on one leg with the other as heavy as lead. But the Majestic One, as usual, let himself be saddled and bridled without giving the slightest trouble.

He only turned round when I tried to mount. He's not used to my crawling into the saddle cursing and groaning. But finally I managed it from the doorstep. And off the two of us set on the road to Salzburg. The Majestic One stepped out as proudly as a Spaniard, for his ancestors were of noble stock from Andalusia. I sat in the saddle with the stirrups slung in front of me, like a broody hen on eggs, for no matter how gentle the Majestic One's elastic gait might be, it jolted my ankle horribly.

I had a splendid riding boot on my sound leg. Only Ambrus Szabo, our regular cobbler in Budapest, can make them like that. But I had stuck a huge felt slipper on my bad foot. It was a good, stout job by Toni, our village shoe-maker, who thought more of durability than elegance. The slipper didn't fit like a glove over the bandage but showed a constant tendency to slide down. So I finally took the thing off and carried it under my arm.

We—the Majestic One, the Hungarian, and I—were well known in Salzburg. But we had never yet passed the Mozart statue or the carillon clock in such a state. I had always hitherto dashed into the post office full of beans. I'd never yet been there hopping on one leg, with a slipper under my arm.

While I was still in the throes of composing a bogus tale of glorious heroism for the Hungarian, the bells started playing "Be ever true and honest." But I refused to be diverted from my inflexible purpose.

I had told a cabman to hold the Majestic One's bridle, but probably the fellow went to sleep. Later on I found the stallion standing up against the garden hedge of the Caril-lon Café. He knew we always went in there. But we haven't got to that stage in the story yet. First I must tell you about the telegram. I spent a good half-hour fiddling about with it. At last I made a fair copy as follows:

Dearest Hungarian,
We are seriously ill. I had an accident with my leg and the Majestic One is being very sticky over his feed. (That last sentence was a delicate way of breaking the news about his gobbling up the rockery.) *It all happened because we were practicing caprioles.* (That was only half a fib and anyhow she would be delighted to hear that we had apparently been able to cut those difficult capers they do at the Riding School; she's been keen on them for a long time now.)

(The wire went on:) *We need your care urgently. Come by return of post. Yours with love, Unholy George and the Majestic One.*

The clerk stared pretty hard when I handed in the telegram, addressed to the Countess Marika Szilády. But he took it all the same. It cost a devil of a lot, so I had to get my coffee afterward on the cuff.

The ride home didn't go off quite so well. My ankle made a terrific fuss. The pain went right up the calf of the leg into my thigh. I had to tell Farmer Lechner, who happened to call just then about winter logs, to see to the Majestic One for me and not bother me about his blasted wood for the time being. I was obliged to lie down again for ages and started wishing things. The priest would have been pleased, thinking I was praying. My wish went as follows:

"O God, see that the Hungarian gets here by the day after tomorrow or the devil will have me!"

Well, that's the prelude to the Majestic One's biography and the relations between the Hungarian and myself that accompany it. And if anyone says it's all wrong to begin a story about a horse and its riders with a broken leg, he doesn't understand the first thing about it and is, moreover, no friend to the truth. When you have to do with horses, even worse things can happen than sitting down in their droppings just because a mare goes by outside and the Majestic One starts trumpeting like a mad trombone player, so that it goes to one's heart and makes one lose the thread of one's discourse in the very middle of a passionate hymn of praise to a pair of beloved beings. It's better to break one's bones than one's heart. A bone can be set. But a man with a broken heart can never be any good for riding again!

2

*A*nother night went by. The hours passed like heavy carts drawn by lame farm horses, with their wheels sticking in the mud of a road across the fields. A man lying sleepless in bed is not a reasonable being. Normally his brief span of life seems to run away with him. He'd like to rein it in, and feels as though he were sitting on a bolting horse. But if he waits and waits and sleep never comes, he doesn't know what on earth to do with his time and wishes he could kill it outright.

Heat streamed in through the open window. It was like being in an oven on that bed-settee. I threw off the blanket. Outside, judging by the many various noises made, much

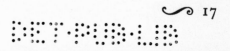

more valuable time was passing. A cats' wedding was going on. It sounded just like a couple of old married people having a row. Every time the two of them started their racket, the nightingale who nested in my garden with his wife stopped singing. As soon as it grew quiet he started off again. The lad's cheerfulness was quite unalloyed. I could have done with some of it.

Later on another song started. That was Korbinian, who owned the water mill. Every evening he filled himself up with wine and came over all musical. As he did three men's work during the day, he soaked up enough for three in the evenings. He always takes good care to send in accurate accounts, does Korbinian. He's a steady sort of chap and knows his own mind, too. Once he fell off the footbridge leading to his mill and dropped into the Salzach. Obviously he must have loaded his wine a bit unevenly that night, for he toppled sideways into the stream. No sooner had he scrambled out of the water than he tried, twice more, to cross the bridge properly. The third time he managed it. His self-esteem, a thing which everyone ought to have, was enormously increased by the fact that he had succeeded in reaching his mill on dry land, so to speak, in the correct manner, despite being soaked to the skin. Yes, Korbinian certainly has a most enviable character. And he would be able to sleep, too, after the wine and his evensong. . . .

The Majestic One didn't seem able to settle down either. I could hear his hoofs on the flagstones outside his stable and soon afterward he appeared at the window and stuck his head in. Its shape gleamed like silver in the moonlight.

"Ay, ay, Majestic One! A nice spectacle we are, aren't we?" I murmured sadly.

He neighed quite softly and faintly, as he always does when he realizes by the sound of my voice that my inner man is in a bit of a mess.

The Majestic One has a great deal of intelligence and sensibility. With him there's no need, as with a human being, to explain one's troubles in words. He knows what's the matter by the mere sound of your voice and if he could help he would do so without hesitation. But it was quite good enough for me that he had just come to look me up and keep me company.

Korbinian was still warbling away:

"Wine, wine, glorious wine!
Never a hat I wore so fine . . ."

Not a bad idea. I happened to have a few bottles of Gumpoldskirchner still lying about, just the right tonic I needed at the moment. But I've always hated drinking alone. Good tipple cries out for good talk. Otherwise there's no fun in it.

So I got up and fetched two bottles. Then I hobbled out into the kitchen again and fetched two glasses. Make-believe's better than nothing.

Then I switched on all the lamps to get a party atmosphere. The Majestic One pricked up his ears and neighed a tone higher than he had before, as much as to say that the plan was a good one and I was well on the road to recovery. "Now then, Majestic One, come along in," I said. "I've had to sit round a table in my time, drinking with a lot of hopeless asses, and couldn't tell them how much I hated them because that wouldn't have been good manners.

Come along in, Majestic One. I'm going to drink with you today, for you're the best lad I ever had as a friend!"

I opened the front door for him and the Majestic One walked into the room.

I pushed the table with the ash trays, the wine, and the glasses over to the settee. Just as I was going to lie down I remembered that the Majestic One also needed some refreshment. So out I hopped again to the kitchen for sugar.

Every time I raised first one glass and then the other, toasting the Hungarian's quick return, the Majestic One received his sugar. He chewed it up slowly, so as to get the full flavor of it, and then tried to wheedle the next piece out of me.

The result was that the basin was emptied at exactly the same speed as the two bottles. Then I passed out. I don't now remember precisely what I said to the Majestic One. All I am certain of is that we woke up the next morning with the lights still on. The Majestic One was lying on the strip of matting. He just gave me one brief look and twitched one ear when I awoke to hear the postman calling through the window. He was brandishing a piece of paper. "Telegram for you," he said. "Come in from Salzburg, it did, a hour agone!"

"And you never brought it till this moment?" I cried angrily.

"Office on'y opens at nine," he growled back. He banged the telegram down on the window sill and rushed off to be the first to spread the news in the village that Unholy George had now gone right off his head with his mania for horses, taking the damned Dobbin to bed with him.

I opened the missive in haste, but with great respect, as I always do with telegrams, and read:

Already in Vienna. If the Gentian holds together will be with you both by the afternoon. Million kisses. Your Hungarian.

"Majestic One, she's coming!" I yelled, springing out of bed on to my game leg. I cursed so hard that the pain actually stopped immediately.

Well, what else could I have done anyhow? A man's got to make a move of some kind when his heart is dancing! The first thing to do was to clear away all signs of our drinking bout; the loaded ash tray, the bottles, and the glasses. Next, to restore order, the Majestic One would have to go outside. So far, he'd neither turned on the hose nor dropped anything. He's thoroughly house-trained, that horse. But he'd have to be groomed. The Hungarian's deadly serious about that sort of thing. She goes over the Majestic One's back against the lie of the hide and if a single speck of dust sticks to her finger I don't dare to look at her.

Well, we were both standing in front of the stable and I was giving the Majestic One his beauty treatment when Mirl turned up. But this time that piece of temptation sent me by the priest couldn't do anything to me. I just asked her to be kind enough to put anything to rights in the house that had got out of place.

I could see by the twinkle in her eyes that the postman must have already passed it on to her that the Majestic One had shared a bedroom with me. Like any other woman, she couldn't resist making a personal remark about it. "So you got so sozzled you took the horse into your room to sleep, eh?" she asked.

"Don't you pretend to be shocked at that, Mirl," I told her. "If it had been you I took, there wouldn't have been much question of sleeping, if I know anything about you!"

"Pooh," she sneered. "I like that! Got your head swelled, haven't you? The sky would have to come down before I came to sleep here at night!"

"I wasn't talking about sleeping, Mirl," I retorted.

She put her tongue out at me and went into the house. A smart girl, that. It was a good thing the Hungarian was coming, so that renunciation was quite easy for me.

I was just combing out the Majestic One's tail, which comes to within two hands'-breadths of the ground, when the priest arrived.

"Weeds never fade!" said he to me with a grin. "But, look here, have you gone crazy or what? Taking the horse into your——"

"Oh, leave me alone!" I shouted, kicking out with my bad foot so that the curse which followed might be a real good one. And, in fact, it turned out such a choice specimen that the priest stood rooted to the spot, quite thunderstruck.

"You needn't use such appalling language," he observed mildly. "I only meant to tell you that the whole village is talking about it!"

"Look here," I said. "If the peasants take their lousy curs into bed with them to warm their cold feet, nobody gossips about it afterward. But when I take the Majestic One, who has as white a soul inside him as he is to look at, into my house, then they jabber like this! No, Father, I'm not crazy, not the way you think I am. I'm crazy with joy! The Hungarian's coming! So there'll be one more home for you with people living together in it who're being a bit previous."

"Oh, so the Countess is coming," said the priest, who's quite used to my unholy way of talking. "We'll be having some good chess then, again."

"Yes, the Countess is coming!" I mimicked him. He's the only one in the village who always calls her the Countess. He's a bit of a snob, is our priest, and drags in allusions to good society whenever he can. But he always has to call a spade a spade with us and sometimes he gets answers that haven't much perfume about them.

"Don't forget to shave while you're titivating that horse of yours," says the priest, who wanted to give me as good as he was getting. But I had my rapier ready for him.

"What's that? Simply shave, Father? Why, I'm going to have a bath, so as to look clean all over, not just in the face!"

"You ought not to talk in that lascivious way, Unholy George," says he. "You'd much better nurse your leg. Mind you take good care of it."

"Oh, rot, Father. True love conquers all things," I told him. After all, it was he who had begun the double-meaning talk. When I reproached him with it, he became fearfully flustered. And when I also informed him that he had no business to send flighty young women into my house, he came down on me like a ton of bricks and said I wasn't even an Unholy George, for the saint had protected the widow and the orphan.

But Mirl, I retorted, wasn't a widow and her parents

were still living, hale and hearty, in Pongay. So his comparison limped on both feet!

The priest wouldn't go on. He believed my impudence to him to be due to my happily excited state of mind. He knows all about us two. Nevertheless, he makes regular attempts to improve us. I wouldn't, of course, let the Hungarian hear me talk so disrespectfully to the priest. She can't stand phrases with double meanings, unless I whisper them to her, but even then they have to be quite decent to listen to, so that she doesn't have to blush. If they aren't, her annoyance makes her even redder in the face and we get near to quarreling.

The next thing I had to do was to take time to make myself respectable, so that she wouldn't again say I was running wild. Sometimes, on these occasions, she takes me, as a punishment, into society in Budapest. Then for weeks on end I don't get a sight of even a horse's tail, not to mention even worse punishments. As soon as I start responding properly to the reins again, she gives me a little more of my head, and then we go off to her estate on the Puszta and run wild together. A grand life that is, with the Hungarian and all the horses!

The priest hung about a bit longer. He gave the Majestic One some biscuits which the animal seemed to want. Then he murmured pacifically, "Praise God!"

"To all eternity, Amen!" I answered, just to please him.

But it looked as though I had said the wrong thing again, for he only shook his white head and walked away.

Mirl leaned out of the bedroom window upstairs and asked if there was anything else I needed.

I stuck my hands on my hips and shouted back, "You

clear out of this, will you? What are you doing up there?"

"The rooms, you fathead!" she retorted.

"Coffee, then, please," I rejoined, touched by so much devotion. She vanished from the window.

The bedroom upstairs, as a matter of fact, was reserved for the Hungarian and myself, no one else. It contained good, honest farmhouse beds and everything was kept in proper order. The chairs and cupboards all had sound legs. They were decorated with carvings by Lois, of Greek mythological subjects treated in Salzburg provincial style. They depicted gods, goddesses, and horses all rioting and reveling together. The priest would have shaken his head over them. But he couldn't have done anything about it. For you can read those stories in the old Greek authors, who knew how to hold down the joy of life by all its four corners at once.

It was a jolly good bedroom, with a stout bolt on the door and the mountains looking in through the window. The atmosphere there was always fresh and clear. As for the beds, with their counterpanes of blue and white checks, you could hardly believe, when you contemplated them afterward, that such innocent and respectable-looking upholstery could be connected with anything sinful. So the big bedroom upstairs was ideally suited for a pair of lovebirds. When the Hungarian was away I slept on the ground floor, on a modern settee that could be turned into a spare bed by manipulating three levers.

Well, Mirl had actually been dusting up there and it was very nice of her. She was fond of the Hungarian and of me, too, though in my case she didn't show her feelings, and a very good thing, too. Well, I gave the Majestic One a good currying and something to eat. He helped himself to a drink. Then I warned him that he had got to keep himself spotlessly clean that day. He would have done so in any case, for that horse is so vain that he avoids all puddles. All the same, I gave him a special lecture that day, so as to impress him properly with its importance.

Mirl had prepared a fine breakfast for me, and as I sat down to it I suddenly felt the devil at work in my ankle again.

"My old man's coming home today, too!" Mirl announced, with sparkling eyes. "He met Marika in Vienna and I've got a telegram, too, I have!"

"Are they traveling together, then?" I asked.

She nodded.

"So we'll be able to wait for them together," I observed.

She nodded.

"It's a bit odd, isn't it," I suggested, "that my Hungarian never said a word in her wire about her having nobbled Lois in Vienna?"

"Well, perhaps she sent the telegram off before she met him," Mirl said.

That seemed to settle the problem. But another question occurred to me.

"By the way, who was it told you I had had a telegram?"

She laughed.

"Who do you think? 'Daily Papers,' of course!"

"Daily Papers" was our name for the postman. You had only to tell him something in strict confidence, swearing him to official secrecy about it, for the whole village to be informed of the subject. If a horse broke wind and he heard the sound he was capable of telling them at the inn afterward that it had been one of ourselves.

But it was now high time for me to resume a more decent habit of thought, as we were expecting the Hungarian. So I dropped dialect and said to Mirl in my purest High German:

"I trust that Lois has concluded his business in Vienna successfully."

She gave me a mystified look and asked why I had suddenly started talking in this high-falutin fashion, as though I had just arrived from Berlin. She was right enough. High German, when spoken the way it was printed, is certainly a polished language. But it's colorless under the surface. When I talk to the Hungarian, whose second home is in Vienna and here, she prefers me to speak just as I think. All I do is to give my natural style a good wiping and scrubbing.

"I suppose you've already put everything to rights over at your place, then?" I asked Mirl. Of course she had. The whole house shone like a new pin and even had flowers in it. The Hungarian was very fond of flowers, too. But with that leg of mine roasting me like a fever, I could hardly have gone out and picked flowers for her.

Mirl went instead, while I got on with my breakfast. After she had come back and put out flowers in the two ground-floor rooms she wanted to go upstairs.

"No, I'll do that," I told her.

"Don't be funny," said Mirl. "Your secrets will be quite safe with me!"

She was in the right. I appreciated, too, the fact that

she had remembered how fond the Hungarian was of flowers.

When she came downstairs again I suggested that until our friends arrived we should keep house together. Mirl could cook lunch for us both at my place. Waiting doesn't seem so long when there's two of you.

"How far do you think they've got by this time?" I asked, when she was already in the kitchen.

"Might be in Melk by now!" she screamed back.

"Oh, rot, Mirl! I'll bet anything they're as far as Linz!" I yelled. I'm absolutely hopeless at waiting for people.

"That 'ud be pretty good going!" Mirl retorted. She's more of a realist and knows that you get on better if you keep your expectations at a low level, so as to be able to rejoice at a high level when the time comes. I suddenly thought of the damaged rockery. The Hungarian would certainly put on her foul-weather face when she saw it. I limped into the kitchen and said:

"Mirl, where can I get hold of a gentian?"

"What, don't you feel well?"

"Don't be silly. I mean flowers, plants, not the liqueur!"

"H'm, yes, that rockery's done for," she said sadly. "But Marika won't blow you up for that when she realizes that the Majestic One trampled over it and you couldn't do anything."

Well, Mirl was right again there, too. All the stones of that rockery fell like a weight from my heart. Moreover, Mirl and I were getting on famously together now. So far not a single sneer had passed between us. We were just happy, each of us, and that was that.

3

The coffee had just come to the boil when we heard a car hoot on the road into the village. The next moment there it stood, the Gentian, the Hungarian's own blue car, with my girl friend and Lois sitting in it. Mirl tore out of the house and I hobbled behind her like a sick stork. "So there you are, George, Unholy One!" cried the Hungarian, taking me in her arms. "How goes it? What's all this you've been telling me?"

Kisses followed. I didn't count them. They were all long ones and we kept our eyes shut, which is always the right thing to do. We couldn't hear or see anything and so never noticed the Majestic One come up till he had pushed his nose in between our kisses. He wanted some, too.

The Hungarian immediately flung her arms round his neck. If anyone thinks a horse can't be glad just like a man can, he doesn't know a thing about them. The Majestic One uttered his most splendid stallion's call and then we were back in the house again, all five of us. The horse joined us in the most natural way in the world. We never realized it till we saw him standing in the room.

"The Spaniards send all their heartiest greetings," Lois told me. It turned out that those two had met, in Vienna, where all kindred spirits always meet, at the Spanish Riding School.

"They want you to look them up soon!" added the Hungarian.

"They've got a hope, now that you're here."

"And how happy I am to be here," she cried, beaming.

Mirl had made some black coffee, such as normally only the Hungarian herself could have prepared. The only one who went for the pastries was Lois, whose disposition has always been a rather practically energetic one. The rest of us were quite content with the mere fact of all being together again. Personally, my only other preoccupation was the question when Lois and Mirl would eventually clear out.

The conversation, however, now turned to my ankle, and despite my desperate resistance I was made to lie down on the settee, where the bandage was untied. The Hungarian went about this business with such a delicate touch that I should have quite enjoyed the process if the pain in my leg hadn't chosen to be so obstreperous.

They all three agreed that the swelling looked positively frightful. The Hungarian decreed that we must leave for Salzburg at once and have the thing X-rayed.

Meanwhile the Majestic One had eaten the entire contents of the sugar basin and the pastry plate. I drew their attention to the fact, hoping for a diversion. But my remarks made no impression on them. The bandage was tied on again and less than five minutes later I was seated next the Hungarian in the Gentian.

Well, it turned out that the bone was seriously fractured. The Hungarian was greatly worried about me. We saw a specialist and he came to quite definite conclusions. He gave orders that I was to keep perfectly motionless.

"Oh, rot!" I said afterward. "The more famous the doctor is, the more dangerous he makes out your illness to be!"

But the Hungarian was adamant that I must stay put for at least a week. Otherwise, she observed, what would have been the point of her coming?

"Oh, I say," I whispered to her. "When we've got everything so spick and span upstairs!"

She bent over me, a half-sad, half-happy look in her brown eyes, and said:

"Don't you think I want you as much as you want me? Come on, Unholy George! Chin up and don't make things too difficult for us!"

A fine state we two have got into by this time! When one of us is happy, the other is bound to be, too. But when one gets a jolt, the other one always has to suffer as well. It would certainly be a better arrangement if love only had its bright side.

The Hungarian refused to allow the atmosphere to grow gloomy.

"Look, I'm going to change now, saddle the Majestic

One, and ride him where you can see us. We'll put the deck chair out in the garden for you and you can watch us go round the ring and tell us when either the Majestic One or myself makes a mistake."

Before I could say a word in reply she dashed outside and heaved her case out of the car. While I was still imagining her standing under the shower, in she came, already booted and spurred.

"Give Lois a whistle," she told me. "So that he can come and help carry you out."

I wanted to hobble out. But she said that if I did the plaster of the bandage would probably break before I'd finished. So I had to whistle from the open window on two fingers, making the ear-splitting screech of a locomotive, twice over. Then Lois answered. He came over at once, too.

I had to hold on to the two of them and so we came staggering out into the garden behind the house. We opened up the deck chair beside the riding ring. We gave the chair a good testing, so that it wouldn't let me down, for the damned thing's mechanism is decidedly tricky.

Soon the Hungarian came by, leading the horse. She said as she passed me, "Did you have a storm down here? The rockery's done for!"

"The Majestic One ate it up and trampled over it, because he was hungry and I couldn't feed him, that first day, on account of my leg," I told her.

The Hungarian had given quite a bit of her heart to that rockery. She was in competition with Lois, who also had one. But now she only said, smiling, "Oh, well! It'll soon grow again!"

Lois gave me a silent look of amazement. She mounted

and put the Majestic One to a walk, gradually persuading him to arch his neck properly and keep his nose a little ahead of the perpendicular. Then they both started off. I say both, for they became inseparable and turned into a single organism. The reins were not held tight. They simply formed a light link between the mouth of the animal and the rider's hands. The Majestic One moved quite freely, in a taut and upstanding style, his gait full of ardor. He didn't buck in the slightest and the Hungarian only bounced gently in the saddle. When she put him into a fast trot, Lois gave vent to his astonishment with a "Gawd stone the crows!" The Majestic One stretched his forelegs out horizontally and kept his hindlegs down in perfect harmony. It looked as though his hoofs might fly off at any moment.

The Hungarian's face was beaming. The Majestic One's eyes were round and glittering and his nostrils wide open. His ears twitched vivaciously, for we ride him more with the voice and with clicks of the tongue than by knee pressure. His mouth foamed as he champed the bit.

They made a marvelously lovely picture, those two, the little, slightly built woman riding the powerful, straining stallion. I forgot my ankle and my longing for my Hungarian.

In the *piaffe*, the pawing movement in which the Majestic One marked time with imposing ardor, they were not quite in unison. He kicked out his hindlegs occasionally, because the Hungarian herself failed to keep time as she helped him. But as soon as he could drop into the dancing step of the Spanish Walk, the measure was well held. He set down and lifted his hoofs lightly and kept a graceful balance with his steps off the ground. I remembered involuntarily how, when I was a little boy, I wept for joy the first time I saw the High School riding style. I fell in love with it at first sight and am as keen now as ever I was.

The final exhibition was that of the *levade*, the Majestic One's star piece, in which he went right down on his haunches and held his forefeet raised, with his forelegs drawn up in a posture of great elegance. He stayed quietly in this pose until the Hungarian sent him forward again with a soft click of her tongue. Another School gallop followed. Then the Hungarian, after a *parade*, let the Majestic One have his head. He then stretched out his legs, relaxing into a stately walk.

"Good work, both of you," I called over to them. The Majestic One got a thump on the neck. Then he stood still in front of me, giving me an intent look. That was a silent demand for sugar. Lois had some in his pocket.

Nearly all of us who live in this village carry sugar in our pockets, for we're all crazy about horses, though I am the only one who will openly confess it. If an earthly paradise for horses exists, it must be here with us in the province of Salzburg, which has been a country of horses since ancient times and still is today. None of our villagers can pass a horse without putting some titbit or other into his mouth. We're goodhearted people in this place, simply because we're fond of horses.

"You'll have to give him a good rubdown," I told the Hungarian, "he's sweated good and proper, the lazy devil."

"You're talking just as though I had no idea how to treat horses, Unholy George," she laughed. "You stay here lying in the sun till I come back. Lois can tell you a story while you're waiting!"

But Lois was shuffling his feet awkwardly.

"Off with you to Mirl," I told him. "She's been looking forward to you ever since this morning!"

Lois, however, pretended he wasn't in the slightest hurry. Well, of course, people don't like to admit they're passionately in love in broad daylight, do they? He muttered something about having work to do, gave me his hand, and strolled casually away.

"Oh, by the way, Lois," I called after him. "I shan't be whistling any more today!"

He made a face at me. I bet he went off at a gallop as soon as he knew I couldn't see him any longer. Lovers like that are perfectly crazy!

Well, we spent another of our lovely evenings and the night was beautiful, full of our stilled passion. But Marika, as we were talking ourselves to sleep, said it was typical of us to have done such a crazy thing. She then formed an important resolution and I had to swear a solemn oath, in conjunction with her, to carry it out. She would spend the whole day with me, we would start quite calmly to retrace the story of our lives, how we first met, how we found the Majestic One together, and what happened afterward right down to the present day. During the narrative my ankle would heal and then we should start going forward in time again and living lives that a beneficent heaven, with a soft spot for both human beings and horses, might be expected to prolong to a good old age. That was what the Hungarian whispered into my ear. Her last words sounded only quite faintly as the breath of sleep bore them away.

4

$\mathcal{I}$t seems superfluous, doesn't it, for me to tell the
Hungarian things she knew perfectly well already through
having experienced them with me? It would simply be a
case of waking up sleeping dogs. I shouldn't be able to say
anything new at all. But I have lived in this village long
enough now to know that novelties are not so easily come
by. The seasons pass by with their old monotonous regu-
larity. First the flowers come, then the fruit. And among
young people here as elsewhere the first night indoors or
out is followed three quarters of a year later by a christen-
ing. And make no mistake about it! If you read or hear
anything that really moves you, it's always something old
and common to all humanity, isn't it? And you only nod

approval, don't you, because you know yourself how often that sort of thing happens to one?

Well, when I began to tell the story of the Majestic One and us two, the Hungarian occasionally put in a word, to remind me of something which particularly appealed to her and which I had forgotten. We hoped in this way to build the tale up piece by piece, till it took shape as a glowing, variegated mosaic, like the one Lois made for the village church. When you look back on life, everything seems to lie in the light of a setting sun that makes even the dark places colorful. So the story we wanted to tell and hear would be a fine one, fine as life itself is at bottom, whatever you may choose to think about it.

At the start of the tale the Hungarian wasn't there yet, so she had to keep quiet while she listened to me and take my word for everything, as I lay on the settee, blowing smoke out of the open window. She sat beside me holding my left hand in both of hers and stroking my fingers.

"Well, then," I began, "one day in May a young man turned up. He had come by train from Graz to Koflach and walked on from there, with a small suitcase, to Piber. He scrambled up the Burgberg, with its four-hundred-year-old castle, its church, the Lipizzaner stud stables, and the houses of the villagers.

"This beautiful district of western Styria has always been a land of horses. That was why it attracted the young man, who was not, as a matter of fact, so very young any longer. The nineteen-fourteen war, which put an end to the Austria of old, had deprived him of all his ideals except his love of horses. He put up at the local inn and found some of the people from the stud there. He discussed technical matters with them and soon they gave up regarding him as a stranger and received him as one of their intimates. Whenever good men meet who are all utterly devoted to horses, they understand one another at once and can spot a rascal the moment he opens his mouth.

"All the afternoon until nightfall they sat together and talked about the Lipizzaners, calling them the noblest horses in the world. The stud people listened with pleasure when the young man informed them that the Lipizzaners had been his most loyal companions during the war. It had been necessary to paint the animals in dark colors to prevent their forming a target for the enemy. Both saddled and in harness they had done their duty as faithfully as any of us. They knew how to die like brave soldiers. And when the young man came to this part of his tale, he lowered his voice and all his hearers stared silently into their wine glasses, deeply moved, as he spoke of the Lipizzaner mare that the enemy's fire had so cruelly wounded under him that in the end she lost her life.

"Then the veterinary surgeon of the stud, who knew everything that was to be known about the horses there, struck his hand through the thick heavy clouds of tobacco smoke that drifted above the table, as if erasing all such dark memories, and told the young man to speak no more of death, but to turn his attention to life, to the eternally renewed life of the horses in the stud. Just then the foals were being born and three were due at any moment. The young man, he said, ought to come and watch the baby horses getting free of their mothers, so that they could start off into their lives on legs of their own.

"The talk had been prolonged so late that dawn took

them all by surprise. At four in the morning a groom came to call the surgeon to supervise a birth. All those present accompanied him.

" 'It's Austria,' the groom said. When they got to her stable, the gallant mare had borne her offspring all by herself. At her forefeet, in the twilight of the stable, lay a still damp and spasmodically gasping lump of horse life. It was a bristly, dark brown stallion, named Maestoso Austria, and destined to be our Majestic One! I edged a bit nearer——"

"I suppose you mean the young man did?" the Hungarian asked.

"Well, of course you knew all along it was me," I told her, and went on:

"I went up and stroked Austria's soft mouth, to give her confidence in me, and then bent over the foal. It raised its head, terribly heavy for it still, for the first steps in life are always of course the most difficult, and looked at me out of its big eyes, with ears erect. I immediately felt as though we two . . . now, how am I going to convey the voiceless language of the heart in words that mean anything to the ear? I felt just the same, you know, Marika, in your own case. I took one look at you and instantly told myself it was bound to be a fine thing if we could pass a part of our lives together.

"That was just what I felt about the foal. I wondered whether the little fellow could possibly have any inkling of what I was thinking. But of course he couldn't. Life must be to him such a miraculously new experience and I could be nothing more to him than one of a number of other strangers. Like all children, he only felt at home with his mother. Well, he must be happy, I thought, to find that he's seen daylight at last. And now, to give him a nice long life, proof against all dangerous maladies, something was done to him that neither he nor his mother could see the point of. He was vaccinated. Then both were left in peace to enjoy their happiness, that of the mother as of the child, the two being always, in fact, identical.

"I asked the manager of the stud whether it would be possible to buy such a foal when it became a yearling and was over the worst of its troubles. But he shook his head, smiling. You certainly couldn't buy Maestoso Austria, he told me. I hung my head in despair. For that was the only one I wanted.

"I next paid a visit to his father in the stallions' stables. A board was affixed to the door of the loose-box giving his name, achievements, and details of his career. The name was Maestoso Nobila, familiar to me from the Spanish Riding School in Vienna, where he had been a *capriole* champion. He was now the pride of the whole stud and destined to be the sire of many famous stallions and gallant mares, demonstrating their maternal heroism in the inviolate peace of the stud farm, as they conceived, bore, and brought up their offspring, in regular succession, to the end of their days.

"Maestoso senior had a somewhat forbidding appearance. Everything about him looked formidable, from his general build to the muscles that rippled under the white, satiny hide. But he was a good-natured fellow at bottom, for he had never in his life come into contact with wicked people, who so easily contaminate others, even the noblest.

"His lips played gently over my hand as I talked to him,

telling him that he was a gallant, noble horse and that Austria had just borne him a son. None of the stablemen grinned while I was speaking, as such wretched and pitiable persons might who have been denied by nature one of her finest sentiments, the love of horses!"

The Hungarian stroked my hand and pressed it to make me look at her. Then she nodded at me, as much as to say that she was glad it was I, of all people, whom she loved. But what she actually said was:

"You know, you really are a sort of Saint George, a queer sort of holy man perhaps. But at any rate the horses can be thankful for you!"

"Aren't you, then?" I asked.

She smiled, blinked at me, and nodded.

"Yes," I said. "The unholy part of it started when you turned up, Marika, you Hungarian, you!"

She gave the skin of the back of my hand a gentle pinch. That was my punishment for being so rude.

"Go on with the story!" she pleaded.

"Well," I continued, "I fell so madly in love with the little Maestoso Austria that I stayed on in Piber. I slept in the big room at the inn. There were two beds in it, one by the window and one near the door. A dark staircase led up to this room, which was situated just under the roof. I only went up there to sleep, however. I was out all day with the Lipizzaners on their pastures. The mares with their foals, the yearling, two-year-old, and three-year-old stallions and mares, all soon grew fond of me. We played games together and the romping black and brown foals would sometimes give me a nip, coming up behind me while I was scratching the others' woolly heads between the ears, where the mane first starts growing. Those foals were a wild, jovial crew. When I tried to take photographs, they would come so near that they filled the whole viewfinder. And the Majestic One was the wickedest rascal of the lot. When I tried to get a close-up of him, he sidled two steps forward, right up to me, and licked the lens till you couldn't see a thing through it for the slime. The more I rubbed it, the blinder that camera's eye became.

"The Majestic One watched me in all innocence. When I scolded him, he really did seem as if he were a bit sorry. How well I know that look today! He pushed his little velvety lips against my sleeve. When he found the buttons at the wrist, he first nibbled them a little with his milk teeth, then seized them. With a jerk of his head he tore one of the buttons off. He chewed at it for a while, till it fell out of his mouth. He spread his legs wide and stretched out his neck while he looked for it in the grass. As he couldn't find it, he tried again to get at my sleeve, which still had two buttons left. I knew then that he was a clever fellow, who would never bemoan his losses but always try to find substitutes. He would probably have eaten every button I possessed if Mother Austria hadn't come up just then. He thereupon discovered that a few draughts of sweet, warm milk were better for him than my buttons. I was able to follow, step by step, the Majestic One's career as a foal.

"For the first few days he still tottered when he stood up and soon got tired of practicing the posture. He would then lie down in the grass again, since it was so nice and warm in the sun. But he soon got tired of that, too. So he would make another attempt to rise. He would stand up as if on stilts and make a few steps. But it looked as though he had to tell each leg what to do before he moved it. However, this struggle with his own legs did not last long. He soon learned how to work them properly. He often skipped as he trotted. And when he came out of step he galloped. That was what he liked best. His legs were still just a bit too long and he had quite a job to prop himself up on them from a lying position. Another trouble was that his neck was too short. The Majestic One would often let it droop in melancholy fashion as he breathed in the scent of the grasses. He couldn't reach down far enough, though he would have loved, for once, to bring his nose nearer to all that stuff that Mother, over there, kept tearing up and chewing. At such times the Majestic One looked as though he were far from satisfied with life. He contemplated the grass with quite a gloomy air. But he would soon toddle off to his mother and suck. His neck was long enough for that and he began to enjoy himself again. The milk was lovely and sweet. It was seasoned with the herbs that grew among the grass of the mountain pastures. The wise and benevolent providence of God is manifest even in the excessive shortness of a foal's neck!"

"Our friend the priest would be very pleased with you if he could hear you say that!" said the Hungarian.

"Oh, him," I said. "He goes quite the wrong way to work. Instead of reprimanding people with psalms and quotations from the Bible he ought to send them out into the horse pastures. They'd soon turn pious then, without his help. When men are left to themselves all they do is to go nosing after iniquity. But where horses are grazing one can only remain virtuous and even become more virtuous than ever. One wanders there over a carpet of grass that never stops growing and has become reconciled to the fact that its sole function, as appointed by God, is to feed horses. And there one has the sky over one's head, with a few clouds about that sometimes pass across the sun, so that the people down below don't have too good a time of it in the warm weather. Sometimes the sky grows overcast and down comes the rain, which is a nuisance to the horses, but is nevertheless quite a sensible arrangement, for it gets rid of the flies and makes the grass grow. Nothing stupid happens in a horse pasture, as it does in a village or town of human beings, where all the inhabitants are quite crazy."

"Yes, but those flies," the Hungarian remarked, "ought not to exist really. When you think how cruelly they sting the horses!"

"Not a bit of it," I retorted, smiling. "Flies certainly are regular brutes, but there's a reason for them, just the same. Because, you know, if there were no such things, a horse would never know why it had such a nice long tail. He bangs away at the flies with it, stamps his hoofs, and shakes his mane. If there were no flies, horses would never do anything but eat and eat. They'd always have their heads in the grass, and their tails would do nothing but hang down and be no use at all for anything but ornament. Oh yes! You must have flies in a horse pasture, that's obvious!"

The Hungarian smiled and yawned a little, for she felt sleepy. But as in the evenings at any rate we never exchange the slightest cross word, she merely said, "Well, now I see why there must be flies in a pasture. But I think, don't you, that you'd better go on with the story tomorrow evening?"

"You're right," I answered. "I was getting tired, too. I should never have been able to think of a more suitable subject to stop at than flies, anyhow!"

5

*T*he following afternoon they hauled me out again
into the garden behind the house, where the Majestic One
was grazing under the fruit trees. Lois and Mirl came along
and the two of them had coffee with Marika at the table I
had put together, though I made rather a mess of it, the
year before. I had my own cup balanced on my stomach,
and didn't dare to breathe. As I had to hold it steady with
both my hands, the Hungarian shoved bits of Linzer cake
into my mouth, though I hate the stuff; it's too dry for me.
They all say, however, that she's a first-class hand at baking
it, so I didn't want to vex her.

The Majestic One also helped to demolish the Linzer

cake. But he always took a mouthful of juicy grass in between the morsels. No doubt he found the cake too dry for him, too. Well, I got thirsty. But just as I was waiting for the last cup from the percolator, the priest chose that particular moment to come slinking through the red currant bushes. He must have actually smelled the coffee brewing. So he got the cup that I was expecting. The Hungarian, to console me, smoothed my hair. But that didn't quench my thirst, if I'm to be quite honest about the matter.

"At any rate perhaps you've a Virginia cigar on you, Father," I suggested. Yes, he had. He's always got some. He finds them much more useful than pious proverbs when he's dealing with the tougher males in the village. When one of their cows has miscarried or the housewife has gone sick, which worries the man less but all the same is very trying, when, in other words, the stricken one requires consolation, the priest always starts off with a few unctuous words. But it's only when he hauls out a Virginia cigar that the consoling words begin to take effect. After that, all affliction gradually goes up in smoke. But it bothers the priest quite a lot to think that a black, withered stalk like that has more effect than the sacred printed word, true as it is that the latter has been put into shape by human agency without inquiry of the Almighty whether the version has His entire approval.

Lois also relieved the priest of one of his cigars and after the holy man (thank heaven) had, furthermore, polished off the rest of the Linzer cake, thus doing me a good turn, we three males each stuck a cigar into our faces. Meanwhile the Hungarian also smoked her usual coffee cigarette. Mirl was the only one who declined the insidious debauchery of the weed. Smoking doesn't agree with her and she doesn't appreciate it either, which is the only reason why many people don't practice habits which they reprove as vices in others.

The conversation turned at first, naturally, to my broken ankle. You would have thought they, not I, had it. I didn't say anything. Then the priest proposed a game of chess. But the Hungarian replied that she didn't feel like it at present. She said she would pay the priest a visit at his house the following afternoon, while I was asleep after lunch. Everyone likes to play chess or tarok or some other game with the Hungarian. The reason is that she knows how to win with modesty and lose with dignity. When she wins she doesn't go into raptures but looks as though she were positively suffering in sympathy with her unlucky partner. She smiles when she loses and says it serves her right. She did tell me once that she didn't find it at all easy to behave so generously, for the fact was that she was only a woman after all and women always find it difficult to keep calm when they play games.

After this, the priest had something to say to Lois. There was a proper Saint George, made of plaster, standing in the church. It showed him pinning the dragon to the ground with his lance, as though the beast were a butterfly destined for someone's collection. My holy cousin and namesake was in trouble. He was gradually falling to bits, day by day. Saint George's next processional ride was hardly likely to be a success. One didn't dare to look at him any more, for fear that a mere glance might make him crumble into dust.

"You needn't beat about the bush, Father," said Lois.

"It's obvious you want me to make a new Saint George for you!"

It was arranged accordingly. The next question that arose was whether the new saint should be carved in wood or chiseled from stone.

The priest considered stone to be too heavy. It would be a beastly nuisance, he said, to carry such an image along in processions. So it was decided that the new Saint George would be made of wood, painted in lovely bright colors, so that it could make a grand impression and please the peasants. The priest's original idea had been that Lois should copy the old saint, the one that was breaking up. But Lois insisted on having a free hand. The priest only agreed to this condition after some hesitation. He didn't altogether trust Lois in such matters. The latter had once carved a Madonna with such a down-to-earth appearance, like one of the village girls, that no one could help licking his lips when he looked at her. Lois, however, reassured the priest. The new Saint George, he said, would be quite respectable.

The priest said nothing more, for Lois was going to provide the new saint absolutely free of charge, literally for heaven's sake. One had to be thankful that he was ready and even glad to do so.

A pause now ensued in the conversation. Someone had to say something, so the Hungarian revealed that, the evening before, I had told the story of my first meeting with the Majestic One, when he was still only quite a small foal. Then the lot of them started bothering me, first one and then the other and finally all four together, to go on with the story. At last I couldn't put them off any longer and had to give in, if only for the sake of peace and quiet.

"Well, then, so I stayed on in the pastures with the mares and their foals," I began. "After a time, Austria, the Majestic One's mother, told him he would have to start using his legs more than he had hitherto. Accordingly, in the intervals of grazing she would set off at a good round trot. Uphill and downhill she went. The Majestic One had to gallop pretty hard to keep up with her. That was how he learned to show his paces.

"But sometimes rows would start. It wasn't only the babies that quarreled. The mothers did, too. Quite often they lashed out with their hind legs and the kicks landed with resounding cracks. Once the Majestic One, in his simplicity, caused a real scrap. He was pushing about on his own among the other foals and mares, when he suddenly felt very thirsty. In his eagerness to quench his thirst he mistook another mare for his mother and made for the wrong udder. The mare first lifted her hind leg, intending to kick his mouth away. But the Majestic One knew all about that gesture. His mother always used to make it when the lad had sucked her udder dry and it hurt her when he wanted more. Well, the strange mare, finding that she could not make the Majestic One understand that he had come to the wrong mother, took stronger measures. She pushed him away and started after him to give him a hiding. Mother Austria had not, of course, lost sight of her son. As soon as she saw that he was going to get into trouble, she came springing, with mighty leaps, right through the grazing herd, while they all looked up at her in astonishment. Austria, neighing loudly, went straight for the other mare. Directly she got close she turned like lightning and gave her adversary one in the ribs. The latter retaliated. The hoofs clashed again and again in attack and defense, till at last Austria's enemy took to flight. The Majestic One's mother rushed after her and chased her round the whole pasture, keeping close to the fence. The two foals, at a loss to understand why their kind mothers had fallen out so terribly, dashed about in utter bewilderment. Austria's thirst for vengeance took some time to satisfy. She did not leave the other mare alone till she had brought her to bay again and given her a flying kick on the haunches.

"Then she neighed to the Majestic One. Instantly he came leaping up to her. Austria flung herself down into the grass and rolled in it, by no means in triumph over her opponent, but simply to brush off the sweat. The Majestic One bounded playfully round his mother. The leaps he made looked as though they might one day develop into school-trained movements according to the old classic rules.

"Peace returned to the pasture. Austria's adversary was licking a small wound in her belly, where the white hide had been broken a little under the kick she had received. But she bore no malice now, not even against the Majestic One, who had begun tenderly sniffing at the filly he had nearly deprived, quite inadvertently, of her milk. The little filly's name was Deflorata and she was a day younger than the Majestic One. They found it fun to be together and before long they were practicing the immemorial foal game of back-lipping. The Majestic One, who had noticed two older foals doing the same thing, tried it out on Deflorata. First his lips played softly behind the withers or over the crupper of the filly. She stood still and did not object even when the Majestic One nibbled her with his teeth and occasionally tugged gently at her hide. After a time the Majestic

One came closer, to give her the opportunity to reciprocate. But he had to nudge Deflorata a few times before she understood what she was to do.

"They played this game of back-lipping for a quarter of an hour at a time. It eventually causes a blotch to form on the back, which is, however, no disfigurement, for foals soon lose their hair, never much to boast of in any case, being so rough and lusterless. In any event, by this time two bald patches have been worn smooth on the haunches by the apology for a tail, that as yet gives no sign whatever of becoming at a later date so magnificent an appendage. At other places, too, the hair begins to fall out. Every transitional stage has, of course, its inconveniences.

"The more hair the Majestic One lost, the greater his desire grew to graze like his mother. He had already sometimes helped himself, on the sly, to her fodder in the stable. But how on earth was he going to reach down to the grass, as his mother did? He tried kneeling, but immediately stood up again, for he felt that the posture didn't suit him, somehow. Fancy him, the Majestic One, on his knees!

"He craned his neck down to the grass again. But it wasn't long enough. Still, a really clever fellow has only to stick to a problem with determination and he will solve it. The Majestic One noticed that he could reach the ground if he spread out his excessively long forelegs. But after a time it became painful to stand like that with one's legs apart. One felt as though one's chest muscles were giving way. He discovered eventually a different pose, that was easier and more natural for him. He would make a proper, really long stride forward and then halt, so as to be able to reach down to the grass.

"It was difficult to bite off the stuff at first. He tore up a whole tuft by the roots, tossed it about playfully as it dangled from his mouth, then gulped it, till he tasted the earth adhering to the roots. He didn't like that at all. So he pushed the whole sample of grass out of his mouth again with his tongue, and told himself that as long as he lived he would never be able to get a taste for such provender.

"But one day he found a certain herb, with tender, aromatic leaves. It had a wonderful flavor. This luxury food led him back to the more usual one. After dessert he turned to a good, plain meal, in other words, grass. That had quite a relish, after all, if you chewed it properly.

"One day I met the chaplain. He was wandering about the pasture like a man who hadn't much to do. 'Well, got your Sunday sermon finished already?' I asked him.

"He laughed, telling me his sermons didn't give him much trouble. They had to be short, because up here the people had nothing but horses in their brainpans. If he couldn't produce any parables with horses in them, no one took the slightest notice of what he said. The congregation's thoughts went strolling out through the church door, which always stood open in the summer, away into the grazing grounds.

" 'They're as horse-crazy as a lot of heathens in this place,' said the chaplain. But he didn't mean that as a reproach to his flock. He was so smitten with the malady himself that he had very likely more than once thought it might be better to be a man of horses than a man of God.

" 'Yes,' I said to him. 'Christendom doesn't pay proper attention to horses. There's hardly anything at all about them in the Bible. I must say that the Gospel narrative would have been a better one if the Lord Jesus Christ had ridden a decent horse instead of that wretched Palm Sunday donkey. But I won't trespass on your territory, Chaplain. I don't mean to pull your leg!'

"The chaplain took leave of me and went his way. He couldn't say anything, because my complaint was perfectly justified. In Christian teaching, of whatever denomination, horses are grossly neglected!"

Deuce take it! I had quite forgotten that our priest was listening! And, sure enough, his blade was out already.

"You may know something about horses," he told me sternly, "but you had better not try to exercise your wit on the doctrines of Christianity. Look up the Book of Job. You'll find something there about horses!"

"Yes, but wait a minute," said Lois. "I wonder whether it was because Job didn't treat his horses properly that the Lord gave his body and soul such a chiseling?"

"I wouldn't have liked to be one of Job's post horses," I interposed, for we were not going to let the priest get away with it now. "And horses are not even mentioned with special emphasis in the Noah's Ark list. If I had been Noah I should have filled the whole Ark with them!"

"You people will never understand anything but horses," the priest retorted. But his defense seemed to be weakening. So I kept right after him:

"The horse, as is his due, has always played an important part throughout the world. The ancient Indians, the Greeks, and the Romans all took horses very seriously in their ceremonies."

"So did the ancient Germans," Lois added. "All their gods were in the Cavalry!"

"And what about Mohammed? He would never have been able to get at the Arabs with his Koran if there had been no reference in it to King Solomon's five mares!"

"A nice example he is, your Mohammed," said the priest. "The very man who preferred to ride asses and camels!"

"Did he?" I asked. "I wonder! You'll have to show me that in black and white before I believe it, Father!"

"I'll lend the Countess the book tomorrow," said the priest. But meanwhile Lois had been thinking out a further line of attack.

"At one time horses were even connected with navigation," he said. "What about the white horses of Poseidon? But navigation's all Christian today and horses have nothing more to do with it!"

"The ancient Germans had their horses of the sun, of fog, and of tempest!" I added.

"Yes, and they were polytheists, too, weren't they?" the priest remarked, thinking that one would unseat us.

"Well, what about nowadays?" I asked. "There are so many saints about that you can't tell one from the other without making a special study of them."

The priest resorted to a trick. He said to the Hungarian, "What is your opinion, Countess?"

That was a silly idea of his, asking her. She never would say a single word against me in front of other people, even if I were wrong a thousand times over.

"Well, you know, Father," she answered, "I simply haven't got one. It was always the men who cracked one another's skulls in disputes about religion. We women were never asked what we thought. All we do is to listen, isn't it, Mirl?"

Mirl nodded, smiling. The priest found himself single-handed again.

"Well, but look here," said he, "you've got Saint George here, haven't you, with his horse? And Unholy George, too!"

It was a highly pacific rejoinder. We couldn't very well deny the existence either of Saint George or my own lack of saintliness. And when there's no denying a fact, we always accept it. We never argue with the priest simply to annoy him. If I were the priest I should never permit myself to join in debate with such harum-scarum fellows as Lois and myself. I should never do anything else but give them my views from the pulpit. People in church don't dare to contradict. They just sit there, listen, look at the crumbling figure of Saint George, and entertain none but the most pious reflections. It would only be if the priest were ever to say anything against horses or the horse-crazy that there would be a murmur of protest. In that case they would never go to church again. But he never did say anything against horses or our love for those most glorious of God's creatures. He did not refrain because he was unwilling to fall out with us, but because he was horse-crazy himself. That sort of thing gets into your blood and he had been longer in the village than we had.

Evening had come on and the priest was the first to think of supper. The Majestic One came and begged him for sugar as he walked off. He gave the horse a pat on the neck and waved his hand again to us as he disappeared.

"You ought not to be always contradicting him," said the Hungarian. "He's such a dear old gentleman!"

"Oh, nonsense," said Lois, laughing. "If we ever stopped arguing with him he'd think he had offended us in some way!"

He and Mirl then also left, whereupon the evening started to be really enjoyable.

We weren't hungry, so we stayed on in the garden. But I didn't want to go on with the story. Marika could see that I was no longer in the right mood. The priest had interrupted my inspiration. But I told her I should be in good form the following day, when we should all three be alone together again, the Hungarian, the Majestic One, and myself, Unholy George. It would be really necessary, too, for us to be quite alone, for Marika would soon now be coming into the story. So I told her, and she agreed.

"We're gradually coming to the point," said she, "when the tale won't concern anyone but just us three!"

6

*T*he Hungarian had brought with her from home a few bottles of the wine grown in the sandy soil of the Bugac district. She now produced them for the first time.

"I say," I said to her, as we were sitting over the first glass, "I'd love to go over and stay with you there again."

"Yes," she answered, "I've been hoping for some time that you would both come over. I'd like to have another foal from Deflorata and the Majestic One."

"Oh, really?" I asked. "And what would you like me to give you?" I didn't look at her.

"Don't be silly," she said. "I want to ride again with you over the Puszta, where we shall only meet herds of horses, oxen, and pigs. We should put up our tent in the evening, the one the pack-horse carries, and watch night fall over the Puszta. Songs would come downwind to us from the herdsmen's camp and we should just hum the tunes, as we're not exactly professional vocalists. What do you think of that for an idea?"

I nodded, muttering peevishly: "But what about my leg? Suppose it doesn't get well soon enough?"

"Oh, nonsense, it'll be all right in a few weeks. I should think you'll be able to move it by the time you've finished the story!"

"Well, if I kept it up all day and all night, we should be ready by the day after tomorrow. But I wonder how my leg would be then?"

"You're talking like a sulky little boy, Unholy George," she told me, giving me a kiss, one of the kind I call soothing. I can't stand them.

"You kiss me as though I were on my deathbed," I grumbled.

But Marika could see that I was not in the least angry with her personally, but only having one of my bad days. I'd been patient for a pretty long time now and couldn't hold out any more. A man turns cranky when for days on end he can get no further than the garden fence.

"How would it be if we went over to Salzburg in the Gentian and read the papers for a bit in the Carillon Café?" she asked.

As I really didn't know what on earth to do with myself, I agreed. I felt like a man who will recklessly swallow any kind of medicine in the belief that it may help him.

So off we went to Salzburg, I wearing my giant's slipper again. Lois packed me away into the Gentian. The night before I had been obliged to whistle for him again, as he had forgotten to bring me in from the garden.

"You won't be back till the evening, I suppose?" he asked.

"We shan't be back till Unholy George has regained his senses," said the Hungarian. "Something has got stuck in him that will have to come out!"

"He's suffering from claustrophobia, I think," said Lois.

"You can go and hang yourself," I told him.

"Something better to do," he retorted. Then Marika drove off.

The Majestic One stood on the other side of the fence and neighed after us. I was sorry for the poor devil, having to stay at home. But nothing could please me that day. A drive like that is of course normally quite enjoyable. But just because my ankle had been smashed up, I felt that I would rather have walked or ridden. I stole a side glance at Marika. But it was obvious I couldn't start a quarrel with her, at any rate not one of those in which one is secretly amused and already looking forward to making it up. Whatever I might say, she would know why it was and be careful what she replied.

I might be able to start a row with the waiter in the café, I thought. But that wouldn't be any good either, because the Hungarian would be there and it would only vex her even if she didn't say anything. If only I were in the saddle, I thought, how soon I could gallop away that psychological cold I had or whatever it was that was eating me. But all I could do was to crouch beside the Hungarian, no good for anything and perfectly apathetic.

If only she would put me to shame, I thought, by asking,

for example, "Do you suppose I came here to gloat over your bad temper?"

But she didn't say anything of the sort. She never said anything at all that could give me real pain even for an instant.

"Shall we drive first to the Cellar Dive," I suggested, "for a beer?"

"That's fine," she said. "Now I'm better pleased with you! If you're thirsty, we shan't be long! You'll soon be yourself again. It's my fault, I think. I ought not to have brought that Bugac in after lunch. Whenever, in an unlucky moment, over there on the estate, I come across those Gentian bottles, I start longing for you two here in the Salzburg country and if I can't get away I'm in the same boat as you are. I know what you feel like, Unholy George, you can't deceive me! We're a regular couple of fools, both of us!"

She took one hand off the steering wheel and stroked my knee.

"I say, mind you don't break some of my other bones as well!" I said, putting her hand back on the steering wheel. I just stroked it once as I did so.

The Hungarian smiled at the road through the wind shield. But the smile was for me really. It meant that we were on the way to making it up.

A little later I said, "Look here, let's go on to Hellbrunn. There will be too many trippers in Salzburg."

"All right, let's go to Hellbrunn," the Hungarian agreed. Her calmness was becoming positively miraculous.

"Look here," I went on, "if I were to say, 'Let's go to the devil,' you——"

"I'd say, 'Let's go,' of course." She laughed. "But what are you in such a hurry for? There's no such urgency about it. The devil will come for Unholy George in his own good time!"

"I don't know what our friend the priest would say if he could hear the Countess talking so recklessly," I observed censoriously.

"And he's expecting me for chess today! But I'd rather he were in a bad temper than you."

"A priest is bound always to keep his temper, Hungarian!"

"I know. Just as a horseman is always bound to be in a vile mood if he can't ride. There are privileges attached to every vocation!"

"What's your particular privilege, then?" I asked, with heavy sarcasm.

"Don't you think it's enough of a privilege to be allowed to be fond of Unholy George?" she retorted. There was a level brightness in her tone, quite innocent of ironic counterpoint.

"Pull up here!" I ordered her in a stern tone.

She put on the brake at once and came to a stop. I gave her the kiss that by now she so richly deserved.

"Now, really, Unholy George," said she, as I let her go, "what are your Grace's wishes? Are we to go to Hellbrunn?"

"What I have said I have said," I answered. "Hellbrunn it is!"

She made the engine hum. We flew along.

I began whistling to myself. She asked, "Why so cheerful all of a sudden?"

"I'm thinking of when we get home, Marika, you Hungarian!"

"But first we're going to drink a coffee in Hellbrunn," said she.

"That's a splendid idea! I should never have thought of that. A coffee always goes down well!"

So the Gentian put its best foot forward to Hellbrunn, though we would both much rather have been going home. But logically Hellbrunn had to come first, now that we had said we would go there.

We drank our coffee in the garden of the Castle restaurant and watched the crowds of inquisitive tourists marching past, armed with their cameras and guide books.

We had once been here years before and seen everything. But at that time there had been only two of us with the guide, as we had arrived at a season when strangers avoid the Salzburg country on account of the heavy showers. It had then been possible to notice that there were actually natives of the place about, not only trippers.

The Castle of Hellbrunn was built at the beginning of the seventeenth century by the Archbishop Marcus Sitticus. I like him, because one is told that he was a great horseman. Het set up two fine stone horses, in the act of performing the *levade*, in the park. On an eminence in the thick of the woods stands the miniature Castle of the Month, with its white upper story peeping out of the green foliage. That odd name was given to it because it took only a month to build. His Grace the Archbishop seems to have been in rather a hurry and got up a terrific head of steam among the artisans. It's a pity we haven't an archbishop of that sort in our village. The wooden spout of the pump at my place has been cracked ever since March. Water comes out of it everywhere except at the outlet where it ought to. But Toni Laderer has hitherto not kept his promise to put it right.

Hellbrunn also amuses me with its fountains, though, to be frank, I don't care so much for the most artistic ones as for those which serve a practical purpose. Among them is a stone table with stools, also of stone, all round it. Their flat seats have innocent-looking holes in them. One might suppose that they were for ventilation, if one could imagine a stone seat ever getting hot. But the holes are put there for a most perfidious object. They spurt water as soon as the proper tap is turned on. Only one of the stools remains dry, that of the archbishop himself at the head of the table. The inventor of so gloriously wicked a practical joke naturally assumed the right to arrange to keep clear of trouble himself. Consequently, the archbishop's guests always knew when they were expected to think of going home. The time came as soon as they felt damp behind.

While I was thinking of this my expression must have been a positively beaming one, for the Hungarian asked me what my inward delight was all about. As I am always quite frank so long as I don't overstep the bounds of decency, I told her I was thinking of the archbishop's stool-fountains.

The Hungarian shook her head indulgently and said, "Aren't you ashamed, when you think of such things, to make faces as though you were reveling in the most delightful memories of love?"

"Oh, Marika," I said, "what piffle! Just ask anybody who has a quiet smile on his face why he is feeling so happy! I'm afraid you'd be a good deal more disappointed than you are with me. My amusement, after all, was only based on the historical fact that certain people got wet behind. And they're all dead and forgotten now!"

"Oh, yes, of course," retorted the Hungarian. "Your appreciation of higher things is sometimes quite uncontrollable! One can't do anything about it!"

"Look here, listen to me," was my reply. "Drive home! And you'll have to pay for the coffee, as you were so absolutely set on our coming here!"

She looked at me as if I had said something utterly incomprehensible. Fancy my blaming her, she must have been thinking, for our coming to Hellbrunn, when I myself had suggested it! But that's Marika all over. She's always ready to take the blame herself and say nothing. I couldn't pay, anyhow, as I hadn't brought any money with me. That's a habit of ours in the village. We go about for days on end without a farthing in our pockets, get credit from one another, and when the time comes to reckon up and pay, there's a row. We have regular rules about it. When it's time for anyone to pay, he wants fun with it. In other places, when people refuse to pay, a complaint is lodged and it's the lawyers who get the fun. In our part of the world a final demand for payment is constituted by a challenge to fight before witnesses. That puts an end to all argument. If our example was followed, the whole apparatus of the law would be reduced to beggary. All the same, quite a performance now ensued. When it came to paying, Marika found she had only Hungarian money with her, amounting to a few pengos. But those Salzburg waiters take a lot of beating. The man looked at the money, told us with great enthusiasm that he had worked for a while, at one time, in Budapest and added that, unless some experience still more wonderful was in store for him, it would remain the most enjoyable period of his life. He then proceeded to inquire whether by any chance the gracious lady happened to be acquainted with a certain Kovacic, or some such name, formerly a waiter at the East Station buffet.

No one who knows my gracious Hungarian Countess could possibly be surprised to hear that she answered that she had known Kovacic, or whatever his name was, quite well. Terribly smart he had looked, too, she remembered, in his black dress coat.

Well, naturally every waiter wears a black dress coat. But mention of this distinctive mark of his profession sufficed to start the two of them off gossiping about Kovacic, or whatever his name was, as if he had been an old mutual friend, though the Hungarian had never set eyes on him in her life. But she wanted to please the friendly waiter and consequently indulged in boundless flights of fancy. In the end the good-natured fellow refused to take any money at all. He said it had been a privilege to serve us. The Hungarian replied that she would also consider it a privilege if he would accept her five pengos. The waiter then swore that he would only do so in remembrance of the gracious lady who knew Kovacic, or whatever his name was, so very well. Both of them seemed positively enraptured at the idea of Kovacic, or whatever his name was, having been a waiter at the East Station buffet in Budapest.

"You ought to be ashamed of having told the poor fellow such lies," I said to her on the drive home.

"It's not wrong to tell lies if you can make someone happy that way," she retorted.

"Really?" I asked. "Then I suppose you've often made me happy like that?"

The Hungarian assumed her characteristic expression of determination. I don't think it suits her. But it was evident from the way she looked at me that the storm had calmed down before it ever got started.

"When a person is in love," she observed, with the solemn air of some long-bearded holder of a Chair of Philosophy, "he's bound to tell lies. Would you have preferred me always to have told you the whole truth, even if I knew beforehand that it would vex you?"

"No, Marika," I answered in a still, small voice, "you're quite right."

I remembered then that the Hungarian had on one occasion done something for me that she had never once mentioned. It so happened that I had got into very low water and yet suddenly everything went right for me again in such an extraordinary manner that I couldn't believe my luck, for as a rule fate is most reluctant to work miracles for me. I once thought of asking her whether at that time, when I was within an ace of having to sell the Majestic One, because we simply couldn't afford either oats for him or a crust for me, she had stepped in, acting as my good angel. But I knew she would disclaim all responsibility, for she refuses to admit that we owe each other anything but our mutual affection and our common love for horses. In her opinion those two sentiments are quite enough to cause two people to stick to each other like leeches. We've tried to separate twice already. But now we've given up the attempt. We no more think of it than we should think of trying to count the blades of grass on the Puszta.

Just as we reached home we saw Lois going across to his house. He was carrying a small trowel. But he didn't turn round, though the Hungarian sounded a mighty blast on the Gentian's horn.

Lois went on walking, as if he had a bad conscience. He didn't look round until I whistled to him, and by then he was already behind his own hedge. He proceeded to behave as though he hadn't seen us for months and months.

"Hallo! Back home again?" he exclaimed. He helped me out of the Gentian. We had no sooner entered the front garden than the Hungarian began to utter cries of delight. Her rockery was in good order again and more wonderful to behold than it had ever been before. The hand of an artist had been at work, evidently.

"Oh, Lois, that was nice of you!" she cried, taking his head between her hands. But Lois took up a defensive attitude, as though he were being falsely accused of some dreadful crime. He didn't do it, he protested. Who was it then? we asked. And what had he been up to at our place, anyhow?

"I was feeding the Majestic One and repairing the door of his stable," rejoined Lois sulkily, as if he had to admit that much, at any rate.

"Oho," I said, "you shut him up, I suppose, to stop him coming out here again and eating up the rockery as soon as you had replanted it!"

"As a matter of fact it was the priest who did it," Lois went on, in a suspiciously disingenuous tone. "Perhaps

Saint George helped him, as you two hit it off so well with the fellow!"

As soon as we were indoors he told us he would have to go, as he had work to do.

That was his way of evading further investigation of the truth. The rascal would have bitten his tongue out rather than confess it. At the front gate he met the priest, who was coming to complain about the cutting of his game of chess. The Hungarian asked him what his explanation of the miracle was, as apparently Lois was not responsible and he, the priest, wasn't either, for anyone could see that he had no black, earth-made edges to his fingernails.

The priest smiled, observing that it seemed as though signs and wonders were still prevalent, if only one were a true believer, as he assumed the Countess to be. We perceived from this remark that one swindler was covering up the tracks of the other, the second one actually roping in heaven itself.

As the priest seemed to have gone to such lengths in the matter, the Hungarian said she was ready to believe in a miracle. She announced her faith with the same air of conviction as she had informed the Hellbrunn waiter that she knew Kovacic, or whatever his name might have been. At the same time the Majestic One stuck his head through the open upper half of the door of his stable and uttered a loud neigh.

"Miracle, indeed!" I exclaimed. "Why, you can even hear the horse laughing!"

The Hungarian and the priest both glared at me, as if I had said something quite blasphemous. Then he started off about the arrangement to play chess. He had even set out the pieces, all ready for the game, he said.

The Hungarian replied that she was very sorry he had taken all that trouble in vain. But she had had to rush me to the doctor in Salzburg, she said, because the pains in my leg had got so bad.

The priest turned sympathetically to me and asked what had gone wrong.

"Nothing," I retorted, "it was all pure imagination."

My answer was at any rate somewhere near the truth. But you can see what happens when an honest man comes into the company of the untruthful, who tell their lies merely to make a good impression on one another.

The priest had only just looked in on his way to old Zenzi at the other end of the village. It was nearly all up with her. But she was fighting tooth and nail for life. Ninety-six was a pretty good score, she had said, but she wanted to reach the hundred mark. The record in the village was ninety-eight, held by the late Pepi Klemperer, whom Zenzi couldn't stand because he had once promised to marry her and then, after her boy was born, refused to hear of any such thing. Pepi had, indeed, paid up. But he had declined to admit responsibility, though afterward, when he was on his last legs, he had bequeathed his farm to the lad.

Well, so the priest went off to Zenzi, with a view to explaining to her that one can't argue about the itinerary planned for one by the Almighty. One has to come when He whistles, and that's that.

The Hungarian wine had disappeared from the table. But the empty bottle still stood there. The saint who had put the rockery to rights must have been fond of his drop. This reminded the Hungarian that there had been something familiar to her about the smell of Lois' breath. She then prepared supper and after we had finished eating begged me to continue my story of the Majestic One.

I said that the fresh air had made me feel tired and that if it was all right with her we could go upstairs and lie down, whereupon I would proceed with the tale.

She looked at me, at first, as though she could hear our sacred oath cracking already. But she then probably considered that her own perseverance in the agreement would be worth something. So she agreed to my suggestion. She went upstairs first and put everything to rights in the bedroom. Then she came down again and helped me up the staircase. It had grown dark in the room. The evening light entered only through the heart-shaped chinks in the shutters.

"I'll be back in a minute," she said, vanishing into the dressing-room next door. When she returned, wearing one of those nightdresses of hers, so cobwebby in texture that you guess they are there rather than see them, I was already lying at full length in bed.

She cuddled up close to me in such a way that I could already hear our sacred oath creak on the way to bending or breaking. But she guided my hand in the direction of propriety and told me I was now to begin my story.

So I sighed till even a dog would have been sorry for me, and started.

"I didn't count the months that flew by while I stayed in Piber. As the weather on the Prentl was stormy, the foals were kept on the Piber pastures all through the summer. It was while the Majestic One was gradually getting used to being independent of Austria, his mother, that you arrived, my Hungarian———"

"Don't skip like that," she reproved me. "Say exactly what happened."

I suppose she's trying to pretend she knows more about it than I do, I thought. But every time I want to criticize her I get stuck.

She gave me a kiss on the cheek and said, "Go ahead! I won't interrupt, so long as you tell the strict truth!"

"Well, one morning, while I was playing with the Majestic One, the stud car was driven down from Koflach and stopped on the road. The driver got out and prepared to help a lady to alight. But she hopped out in a moment and crawled right through the wire fencing like a jump-shy mare.

"She came across to me over the pasture and I noticed that she had a camera with her. Oho, I thought. Another of those women news hawks come to visit us! We can expect another of those sentimental illustrated articles that make every horseman shudder the moment he starts reading them.

"The driver came running up behind her. He introduced her to me by saying, 'This is Her Ladyship the Countess from Hungary!' He didn't mention my own name, perhaps because it hasn't got a handle. Only cabmen call me Baron.

"I raised my hat. She nodded.

"I took a firm hold of the Majestic One's neck. I would much rather have picked him up in my arms and bolted. So long as she doesn't actually put her hands on him, I thought jealously.

"I certainly liked the look of that Countess. She wasn't made up or dressed in any silly new fashion. She wore a blue hat and very dark brown curls peeped out from under it, so dark that they might have been thought black. She also had on a gray weatherproof coat of precisely the right kind for encountering sudden showers.

"The driver departed abruptly. We stood there together, without uttering a word. All she did was to click her tongue to the Majestic One and hold out her hand to him. It was a beautiful little hand, as those who envied it no doubt admitted.

"That scamp of a Majestic One actually started pushing and shoving forward under my arm. But I wouldn't let him go. Love me, or I'll use force, I thought. He ducked backward, though, and got away from me. He made a few jumps round behind me and then there he was with the Countess, who at once began stroking and squeezing him as if she had never seen a foal before in her life. She was laughing aloud at the same time, to see me standing there alone, abandoned by the faithless Majestic One. I had half a mind to call him back, but decided not to. He probably wouldn't come, the rascal, and I should look more of a fool than ever. It's not so easy, I thought grimly, to entice any one away from arms like that. I was at a loss to know whether my rage was mostly envy of the Countess because of the foal or jealousy of the foal because of the Countess.

"I got into such a muddle that I felt sure the Countess must notice it. But she remained perfectly oblivious of the storm that was rising within me. She was far too busy with the foal.

" 'Will you be staying here for some time?' I asked, for the sake of saying something.

" 'I don't know yet how long I shall stay. But it will certainly be for some time,' she answered.

" 'How comes it you talk as though you were one of our-selves? I'm afraid I don't understand a word of Hungarian.'

" 'You don't have to, since I speak the same way as you do,' she retorted.

" 'Then I suppose you——'

" 'That's it,' she said. 'I lived in Vienna for many years before the war and I come back every year in the spring.'

"Well, I was pleased to hear that Hungarian Countess say such a thing. And when the Majestic One pulled one of the buttons off her coat I didn't have to force myself, any longer, to be agreeable.

"Look, he's undressing you! You'll soon find yourself standing out here in the pastures like Eve in paradise!' I said, laughing.

"The Countess turned red.

" 'I'm sure you realize I only meant that in fun?' I added."

At that point the Hungarian interrupted me, observing: "Well, Unholy George, when you said that, I knew you were in love with me. You pulled such a face! It looked as though you were genuinely sorry for having made such a silly joke."

"It wasn't so silly as you think, you Hungarian!" I rejoined.

"But you also looked as though you'd really have liked to see me as Eve! You put on such a covetous expression!"

"And do I ever look like that now? I'm sure I don't mean to, Marika," I exclaimed, for I don't care about showing that 'covetous expression.'

"You don't nowadays, for the simple reason that you

don't need to. But it's not because you've improved, as you seem to imply!" she retorted.

"Well! So you knew, even then, that I was in love with you?" I continued.

"I don't tell lies, do I, Unholy George?"

"What about Kovacic, or whatever his name was, then? You said you knew him! If you're telling the truth now, it means you guessed I was fond of you before I guessed it myself!"

At this point the Hungarian again had to call me silently to order. But she didn't do so as decidedly as she had the first time. When I resumed the story, I was quite unable to suppress my inward exultation.

" 'So I suppose, gracious Countess, that you will be staying at the inn?' was my next question.

"She nodded. But she did not seem positively enraptured at the prospect. I smiled.

" 'What are you grinning at?' she asked.

" 'From delight, of course!' I answered. 'There's ónly one inn at this place. It has only one guest room. And that's mine!'

" 'Well, you'll have to look round and see where else you can sleep,' she instructed me calmly.

" 'I say! That's not very flattering to me, is it?' I exclaimed. 'Allow me to explain, if you please! There are two beds in that guest room, I may tell you. And they are quite a long way off from each other. Only just within hailing distance, so to speak.'

" 'So far as I'm concerned, you can sleep where you like!' she retorted, masking her annoyance with an indifferent tone.

" 'It's true they've a billiard room,' I said. 'But if it's all the same to you and you care to leave it to me, I should prefer the guest room to the billiard room——'

" 'Oh, do be quiet!' she fairly shouted at me. She looked pretty, standing there in such a rage.

"Meanwhile she had let go of the Majestic One. He came over to me and placed himself at my side, as if he meant to say, 'It would be funny, wouldn't it, if we two couldn't get the better of that Hungarian Countess?'

" 'Well, we've plenty of time to decide before the evening,' I remarked, to calm her down. Then she came and tried to get the Majestic One away from me again. But just then he happened to want to stay with me, because I was rubbing his left-shoulder joint, which was his favorite spot. So she started stroking him elsewhere. But a four-month-old foal is not an elephant. Our hands, accordingly, happened to meet. I took the opportunity to stroke, by sheer accident, her hand instead of the foal's hide. She kept her hand still, too, for a second."

"But I wasn't in love with you, Unholy George," the Hungarian interrupted in a severe tone. "I was angry at what you had said about sleeping and the billiard room. 'He's just the same as all the other men,' I said to myself, as a matter of fact."

"But you did come to appreciate my good qualities later on, Hungarian," I said, taking her in my arms.

"I don't know about good qualities," she said. "Heaven only knows what made me fall in love with you at that time. And now just you leave me alone and go on with the story!"

"Well, then," I went on, "so you took your hand away.

And when I caught hold of it a second time and hung on to it, you snatched it away, giving my own hand a slap."

"Yes, and I felt dreadfully sorry I had done it when you stared at your hand in such an idiotic way. So I apologized. But look here! You needn't expect me to now!" she interrupted again.

"That's too bad of you, Hungarian," I rebuked her. My stalking hand had reached a new position undisturbed. But in case she should suddenly notice it, I went on rapidly:

"Yes, so then we arrived at the village inn about noon. But it's not enough simply to say we arrived. You had sprained your ankle in a hole made by the horses in galloping about the pasture. And it must have hurt a lot, because you took my arm and so we arrived at the inn with you leaning on me for support. When Reserl, who managed the inn for her old mother, saw us come in like that, she exclaimed that she had been quite right after all to have taken the gracious lady's trunk straight up to the gentleman's room.

"You didn't make any comment. In the case of any other woman I should have been sure, then, that everything was going to be all right. But not in your case, you Hungarian! You were different from everyone else even then!"

I started a gentle stroking movement with my hand and she pretended not to notice it. So I continued to relate my story in a rather roguish fashion.

"Well, we ate lunch together and told each other anecdotes about horses and now and then about ourselves. At last you told me to stop calling you Countess all the time. 'Gracious lady' was another form of address you said you were sick and tired of by the time——"

"By the time I had found out that you were just as hopelessly crazy about horses as I was!" The Hungarian helped me out with the phrase, changing the position of my hand back to her shoulder.

" 'My name's George, in case you ever want to call me,' I told you, then. You informed me in reply that you would have no objection to my calling you Frau Marika. We were already sitting over our wine by that time. The wine had worked so well by the afternoon that you never noticed that I was regularly calling you plain Marika. That afternoon, too, the mares and foals had left their loose-boxes again for the pastures. During the hour of noon itself the flies out there are much too troublesome, so the horses are stabled for the time being. They made a pretty sight, seen from the window, which had a view of the road down. It took a turn away through the ancient trees, the white hides of the mares gleaming between the green foliage. The sight was so beautiful that you leaned against me and never noticed me give you the lightest possible kiss on the neck."

"I did, though!" said the Hungarian.

"You really must stop spoiling all my effects like that, Marika!" I cried. Then I went on:

"Well, so then we went out to get some fresh air in the pastures. Your ankle was all right again by then. . . . And I say, by the way, was that ankle of yours all a pretense or did it really hurt so much?"

"I'm not going to spoil any more of your effects, Unholy George!" replied the Hungarian. She trapped my hand and pulled it back to her shoulder, where she considered it couldn't do any harm.

"That evening, however, the great decision had to be

taken. Over dinner we had a consultation. You told me that in your opinion even that billiard room would be better than no bed at all. I replied that we ought not to attract any attention and bother Reserl by proving that her connoisseur's eye had been so mistaken in our case. We discussed the whole affair quite seriously after dinner, over a few glasses of wine. Suddenly you came to a heroic decision and imposed your conditions. In the first place you were to precede me upstairs and I was only to follow half an hour later. Secondly, you were to have the bed by the window, so that I should not have to pass in front of you and you would be able to call for help from the window if necessary. Thirdly, no light was to be allowed. Fourthly, snoring was forbidden. Fifthly, I was to give my word of honor as a horseman not to assault you while you were asleep. A supplementary regulation enjoined that in the morning I was to keep my head under the blanket so as not to see or hear anything when you got up. A very special point was made of this procedure, as part of that covered by the horseman's word of honor. Well, by this time I was prepared to put up with anything and in any case one ought to be thankful for even the very slightest improvement in one's prospects. So I pledged my word of honor as a horseman and swore, into the bargain, that I would keep my word now that I had given it. After this, we went on talking until far into the night. In the end it was not until after midnight, Marika, that you fell asleep. You had previously complained of being cold in bed but had begged to be excused from accepting my offer to come and help you to warm up. You said a tot of schnapps would be a more reliable expedient.

"The last question you asked was whether I was very fond of that colt, the Majestic One. Yes, I was very fond of him, I answered. You didn't say anything more.

"When I woke up the next morning you had already flown. You were sitting downstairs at breakfast.

" 'George,' you said, 'from this day forward I decree that you shall be known as Saint George!'

"I retorted that a saintliness which required mortification of the flesh on such a scale was of no possible interest to me. I added that my word of honor had only been given for a single night and that I should have to consider very seriously whether I could be justified in renewing it, in that reckless fashion, on any subsequent occasion. Most of the saints, moreover, had always taken good care to begin by enjoying the things they afterward renounced. Saint George, I pointed out, had been no exception to this rule.

"Finally, however, breakfast seemed more important to me than all the empty airs of my new sainthood.

"Later on the stud manager's assistant asked whether we would like to see the Majestic One's father at exercise.

"It was raining. Only a slight drizzle was falling. But the sky did not seem likely to clear. The stallion Maestoso was therefore given his exercise in the covered riding ring. He was saddled and bridled. One of the stud grooms sent him round the ring on the lunging rein.

" 'I wonder if he can still remember any of the tricks he learned at the Spanish Riding School?' you remarked to me.

" 'What you really mean is that you would like to know whether I can ride,' I rejoined. I went over to the man with the lunging rein. At first he was reluctant to let me ride the stallion, as he was responsible for the animal. But at last I managed to persuade him.

"Old Maestoso made a tremendous fuss at first. He wanted to find out, to begin with, what sort of rider he had got in the saddle. But as soon as he discovered that I knew the ordinary ropes pretty well and also had some idea of trick riding, we understood each other. First we went through all the usual paces. We put up a good show, prancing in the *piaffe* and the Spanish Walk. And that, I thought, would be enough. But you called out to me that Maestoso had been famous for his *capriole* in the Spanish Riding School and suggested that I should try and see whether he could still do it. I really got a bit warm then in the saddle. A high jump of this sort, with the horse kicking out behind as well, till you feel he's going to split in two, needs a stout heart, I can tell you.

"I did know one thing about it and that was a piece of luck for me. Maestoso had been trained in the Spanish Riding School by a friend of mine, Leopold, the senior master. I had got to know the way he handled the horses.

"Accordingly, I put Maestoso into the *piaffe*. And as soon as he was keeping good time, with his haunches steady, I made him rear for the *pesade*, then, with a click of the tongue, sent him out of it in a lightning leap. As he jumped I gave him another click of the tongue and a pressure with the thighs. He extended, jerking me from the saddle. But I stuck on, though the intake of his breath nearly forced my thighs apart. I got another jolt as the stallion came to earth again on all fours. Then the *capriole* was over. I hadn't quite sat it out. But at least I had stood it out. I was out of the saddle in a second, making much of Maestoso. He had done the best he could and had treated me with every consideration.

" 'You deserve a piece of cake for that, Saint George!' you told me joyously. 'But don't cram it all down your throat at once!'

" 'When a man's heart is full,' I answered, quite seriously, 'his mouth is apt to get full, too. You know well enough, Marika, what I should like to have!'

"You said gently, 'Go on being Saint George for a while yet. You'll lose your sainthood soon enough. I'm afraid your patience won't last much longer!'

" 'Well, what I want next is that son of Maestoso here, the little Majestic One. I'm so fond of him! But they won't sell him and I'm afraid, Countess and Hungarian though you are, that you can't help me in that case either.'

" 'Oh, that's what you want, is it, Saint George?' you asked. 'The foal, eh?'

"I nodded, gloomily enough.

" 'Well, well,' you said, 'we'll just have to see what we can do in that direction.' "

The Hungarian snuggled up to me and I tightened my embrace. "Tell me," I asked. "Why didn't you grant the first of my wishes at that time, which was for you yourself?"

"Just because I did want to grant it. It was my own wish, too. You never realized then, did you, stupid, that I meant to give it you? You were to have the woman and the horse as well! And that'll be enough of the story for today, Unholy George!"

Marika wasn't tired. But she was in so enchanted a state of waking dream that the solemn oath which we had kept so well for a few days was getting lost in the dark depths of memory. It had positively passed into history. Time had caught it up.

As we were on the point of falling asleep, the Hungarian said in her warm, deep voice, "I'm going to swear to you now that I'll never take another oath that involves us two!"

7

The love between the Hungarian and myself is subject to palpitations of the heart. It's not that either of us doesn't trust the other. But—well, I have often wondered, sitting alone on the bench in front of the house and listening to the Majestic One snorting in his stall, what gives rise to these palpitations. It will be clear to anyone, from our story so far, that we are neither of us of an age generally supposed to be youthful. But, of course, in love that really doesn't count. So far as lack of sense is concerned, we outdo even the youngest. Naturally, the blood doesn't boil over into our senses any longer. In our case it flows to the heart, which then experiences its own tenderness, thus providing a counterpoise to the heightened pressure. We have never felt, when together, what our friend the priest condemns as sensuality whenever a premarital increase in the population again occurs in the village. We have spent quiet hours in each other's company, when restraint has been enough, of itself, to make us happy. It may be that compromise comes easier to people who have much to do with horses, that a light hand on the reins means as much in life as in riding. When the Hungarian rides the Majestic One, as she had to while I was laid up, thoughts occur to me which are more easily committed to paper than spoken. She uses an infinitely light hand, no compulsion at all, the mere stimulus of gentle movement, to persuade the Majestic One to perform. You can see by the look of him how much he enjoys following the lead of such a woman.

My own hand works harder, of course, and I urge him forward more vigorously, when I ride him. I have the feeling, each time, that it is necessary to persuade the Majestic One to give me willing obedience. With the Hungarian in the saddle his gait is easier. The silent music of his movements is then a kind of improvisation in which one takes a special pleasure in the slight errors and caprices that occur. But under me the Majestic One has to work. We never overlook each other's mistakes. He reacts to mine instantly and I correct his. Before the two of us achieve perfect mutual rhythm, the sweat fairly runs off as we labor to render the performance a satisfactory one. But we don't perspire in the effort to make one or the other yield or collapse. We don't fight a duel in which one wins and the other is defeated. On the contrary, we strive to work in harmony together. I use my head when I ride the Majestic One. The Hungarian employs her unerring instinct, which brings her closer to the horse's own feelings. In my case, however, he relies on reading my thoughts. It is quite a little while before he becomes letter-perfect in that process.

The Majestic One, in an odd sort of way, plays the part of an intermediary between us two. He has taught us to feel in the *haute école* fashion. Whenever I rode him in the morning, with my head still full of Marika, he moved delicately, as though he were carrying her. But as my memories of the woman I loved ebbed away, his gait grew more and more emphatically that which he only adopted when I rode him.

The *haute école* of horsemanship and of love came to mean the same thing for us. If this statement seems unintelligible, well, all the trouble I have taken to make things perfectly clear has been in vain. I invariably come to grief when I take to cold logic. No doubt my heart is often too much for my head. If so, it's all the Hungarian's fault, for I have come to resemble her, now that we have grown so intimate. People are attacked by logic, she says, as the years roll on, just as they are attacked by gout. When the soul grows cold it catches the infection of logic at the same time. But we two are immune from colds in the heart, for our palpitations and our lives together enable us to keep each other warm.

When I explained all this to the Hungarian, she said my last idea was the best of the lot, though some of the rest, no doubt, weren't bad, if only she had been able to understand them. They went a bit beyond her, she observed. What the kindhearted creature really meant was that they were too intricate and confused.

She took the blame herself for the chaos of my thoughts.

It was her fault, she said, for bothering me to relate our story. To this I replied that it was necessary even for me to say something obscure occasionally, just to give the narrative the appropriate air of profundity. The less people understand anything, the more they admire it. If they ever did succeed in deciphering the decrees of the Almighty, it would be all up both with His grandeur and their own human happiness. It's a good job those decrees of His are inscrutable and that we all have different ideas of what He is like.

The Hungarian and I, however, both see Him in the same way. Our God is a youthful, knightly figure, riding a proud steed. So we feel on quite familiar, intimate terms with Him. The consequence is that to us riding is a sacred ritual, relieved of its solemnity by the inward joy felt in the practice of any art.

Our priest once saw us ride a *pas de deux* at a festival in Salzburg, held in the Rock Riding School. He told us afterward that we had looked positively devout. His voice sounded rather melancholy. He seemed to be regretting, in a quiet way, that we did not assume such expressions while he was interpreting God's word in church. I expect that on those occasions we looked like children at school who can't understand the teacher but just say to themselves indulgently, "Preach away! We know better than you do what's good for us!"

All through the day after the night when we had broken one oath and sworn to keep another we were in a mood which the Hungarian called, in her amiably derisive way, an elevated one. It didn't even relax when we examined the Majestic One's latest dung and unanimously agreed that it was highly unsatisfactory. He must have got his teeth into some powerfully aperient kind of plant in the pasture behind the house. The Hungarian had immediately gone to investigate. She's an expert on horse fodder. But she couldn't find anything. The Majestic One had made a clean sweep of his grazing.

I was just examining the midday menu, which included Tyrolean dumplings, when the Hungarian suddenly pushed the stable shovel, full of normal horse droppings, through the window, exclaiming gaily that all was now once more well with the Majestic One. The Tyrolean dumplings certainly tasted a bit mushy owing to not having been kept under proper observation. But in compensation we did have quite healthy horse droppings. The other way round would have been all wrong.

The Hungarian now felt so magnanimous that she was determined, she declared, to perform a good deed. So I had to lie down to sleep while she went to the priest's house to play those overdue games of chess. At five o'clock she still hadn't returned. But round about six she turned up, beaming. She told me the priest had won all four games. It had been quite a struggle to insure his four victories, because he always, out of courtesy, tried to arrange for her to win. He had studied every move with deep attention, in order to find out the best way of getting into trouble. It's not much fun, of course, playing chess with the priest in these circumstances, because the Hungarian can't swear, which she loves to do when she and I play together.

In our own variety of chess the main thing is to prevent anything happening to the knights. At the end of the game the one who has brought them safely through all dangers is adjudged the winner. We regularly take each other's kings, which, according to the rules, is an outrageous proceeding. Lois says we absolutely ruin the game with our horse-craziness. But that's the way we like to play and it has nothing to do with anybody else.

After dinner we were again due to go on with the story. But neither of us was in a hurry to do so. For we now had to deal with a most tragic incident in it.

"Well?" I asked, at last. "Shall we go on or not?"

"What's worrying you?" she demanded.

"Look here," I said. "I'll make a start and when we come to the hurdle we'll just send our thoughts sailing over it!"

As she didn't answer I went right ahead:

"Well, after that morning in the riding hall at Piber we went out into the pasture, as usual, to visit the little Majestic One. He was already standing just inside the wire fence and neighed when he saw us coming. Mother Austria also neighed, but in a low, uncertain tone, as though she thoroughly disapproved of her son's attachment to those two human beings. When we ducked under the wire, she came up to us with her ears laid back. She pushed the Majestic One aside. He bounded off a little way, then stood still and shook his short, erect mane. He couldn't understand why his mother didn't like us.

"Austria stood in front of us, on guard, twitching her ears. We walked slowly up to her.

" 'Good girl, Austria,' you said kindly. The mare's anxiety gradually grew less tense. The jerky movements of her ears slackened by slow degrees. When we reached our two hands out to her, with their familiar, reassuring, horsy smell, the ears suddenly remained motionless, pointing forward. Her nostrils quivered. Austria advanced a pace with her forelegs, leaving her hind legs where they were, and stretched out her neck. A moment later we both simultaneously clasped it.

"She rubbed her muzzle against your shoulder, allowed my hand to rest between her ears, dropped her head still lower and drew in the hind legs she had been keeping at a distance. We made our peace with the mare and then the Majestic One, too, trotted up on his stiff legs. He made for the udder and began to suck. His decision was taken. He belonged to Mother. Our caresses were certainly agreeable. But they didn't strengthen him. Moreover, his weeks as an unweaned foal could now be counted on the fingers of one hand. The intention was, in fact, to take him from the mother sooner than the other little fellows, for he was exhausting her with his thoughtless and childish craving for life and growth. The young mare's first born was taking it out of her. The time was approaching when she would have to assume her arduous duties as a mother, involving the production of one foal after another.

" 'Are you going to stay?' you asked. 'I'll have to go to the house now.'

"The day before, I would have let you go and been glad to detach you from the Majestic One. But now things were different between us. I went with you toward the house.

" 'Don't you feel well?' I asked.

" 'Of course I do!' you replied. But your voice didn't sound very steady.

" 'Look here, what's the matter?'

" 'Nothing, Saint George! I just want to be alone in the room upstairs, that's all. I'll be back directly.'

" 'No sooner do we begin to understand each other than she wants to be off on her own again,' I thought bitterly. I remained silent.

" 'I suppose you think I'm being sulky now?' you inquired.

"I shook my head, like a man at his wits' end, who doesn't even know what further questions he ought to ask. As we entered the inn you said to me:

" 'Give me a kiss, Saint George! And then go and see if those last two foals have been born yet.'

"I forgot about the kiss and only asked: 'Whatever's the matter, Marika?'

" 'Nothing! You're such an innocent, it's positively fascinating! Off you go now. Wait for me, I'll be back quite soon, really!'

"I gave up trying to make head or tail of it then. I did as you suggested and walked along the path beside the inn, leading to the stables. I kept wondering what on earth I could have done to offend you and could think of nothing. I never realized the situation until, after an eternity of more than half an hour, you came back and started making fun of me for having missed that first kiss out of sheer silliness. You seemed to be in the highest possible spirits, as though you had never sent me away at all. But still I didn't feel properly at my ease. I had always believed that no good can come of it if a woman chops and changes like mountain weather."

"I liked you at that moment," the Hungarian interrupted. "You were taking it all so seriously, thinking that something must have gone wrong between us two!"

"Shall I stop now?" I asked.

"Oh, no, Unholy George! I'm quite keen now to hear the rest of the story!"

So I sighed deeply and continued:

"So far as I was concerned, the whole day had now been absolutely ruined. And when, that evening, you said you didn't want any wine, I thought that the end had come for us two before we had fairly started.

"Shortly afterward you announced that you wanted to go upstairs again. I asked, accordingly, where I was now expected to sleep. You took me by the left wrist then and said: 'Listen, Saint George. As soon as the big hand points to ten, you come up, too!'

"This time you didn't ask me to give any horseman's word of honor. I was simply to come up. She's lost interest in you now, I told myself, after you had gone. And I stayed downstairs, moping, till the big hand moved a long way past twelve.

"All the same, I did go up then. I entered the dark bedroom very quietly and undressed. When I lay down, the bed creaked and I got a fright. Then for a time I could hear nothing.

"'Aren't you going to say good night to me, Saint George?' you demanded, rather plaintively.

"'Good night,' I answered, putting a heavy sigh into my tone.

"'Won't you come over and give me a kiss?' you went on. I got out of bed. It was all the same to me now whatever further incomprehensible things might happen. The bed squeaked and groaned in apparent relief at getting rid of my weight. I had to grope my way over to you, for it was pitch dark with the shutters fastened over the windows. I stubbed my bare toes against a piece of furniture. Touching it with my hand, I found it was your bed.

" 'Come and sit down,' you said. 'Did you hurt yourself?'

"I felt for the extreme edge of the bed and squatted down on it.

" 'Give me your hands, Saint George,' you said, taking them in your own as you spoke.

" 'Now don't be angry with me,' you added.

" 'I'm not angry with you, Marika,' I answered. My voice had grown so hoarse that the words almost hurt me.

" 'Tell me, Saint George. Have you come to the conclusion that I'm a freak? I'm only a woman, for all that!'

" 'Yes, of course,' I replied, not being able to think of anything more brilliant to say.

" 'Well, there you are, then! Now, will you promise to believe every word I'm going to tell you?'

" 'I'll try, Marika.'

" 'Come nearer to me, Saint George. Then I shan't have to shout so. Now look here, I'm very fond of you and I should like to . . . don't you understand?'

" 'I'm very fond of you, too, Marika. But I still don't understand,' I said. I had no idea what she was talking about. 'What is it you want to tell me?'

" 'That I've been longing for you all day! That I'm so glad you're here! I should like to have been still more glad. But it's no good.'

" 'Has something happened, then, Marika?' I asked, feeling desperately anxious.

" 'Yes, Saint George, it has—at the wrong time, too!'

"I understood then, and found I was blushing.

" 'Marika, don't be angry with that fool of a Saint George!'

" 'On the contrary, that's just the reason I'm so fond of you,' you answered. 'Give me a kiss and stay here till I go to sleep!'

"That was when I first kissed you, my Hungarian. And when I gave you two more good-night kisses, one on each eye, the left had a forlorn little tear trembling in it."

"Fancy your remembering that!" cried the Hungarian, in great delight.

"I realize more than that now," I answered. "Your love for me had got you into such a state that even your dates had got all mixed up. . . ."

"Now then," the Hungarian said, torn between her respect for the conventions and her amusement at my belated recognition of the facts, "it's high time, you know, to stop storytelling for today."

"Quite right, Hungarian! I feel positively shattered! It was really tragic, that episode!"

"I feel quite shattered, too, at your resourcefulness in hitting on just the one word that gives the whole game away."

"Now don't start quarreling with me in the middle of the night, Hungarian!"

"I wouldn't dream of such a thing, when you're so clever with words!" she retorted, shaking her head.

It gradually dawned on me that fate, in the end, had

made rather a mess of that whole beautiful and deeply tragic story. When I admitted as much to the Hungarian, she replied, in a tone suitable to the repose of evening, that only the best of men are always so ready to acknowledge their mistakes.

8

*N*ext morning Lois turned up and said he would like to make a start on the statue of Saint George. He intended to make it a life-size work, in wood, put together from a number of different parts.

"All right," I said. "Go ahead and make the shavings fly! The figure of Saint George need not be modeled so very precisely. If one arm comes out shorter than the other, nobody is going to notice it. But you'll have to be careful about the horse. If anything goes wrong with him, the villagers won't let the new Saint George inside the church. They know a darned sight more about horses than they do about pious legends."

"That's the reason I want to work from a model," Lois

rejoined. Then he blurted out that he would like to use the Majestic One, Unholy George's horse, to make Saint George's horse. Not only this, but could I mount the stallion and put him into the *levade?*

"Do you mean to say, then," asked the Hungarian, "that you want Unholy George to pose as a model for Saint George? The Almighty must have the patience of an angel if he ever permits such a farce to be perpetrated in His name!"

There was a further point that Lois had in mind. He observed that Saint George was not only a dragon-fighter, but also a protector of widows and orphans. To cut a long story short, he meant his Saint George to be running the dragon through with the lance in his left hand, while with his right he would be holding a young woman seated on his saddle-bow. It wouldn't matter, said Lois, whether the young woman were a widow or an orphan. But he did consider it important to have the Hungarian as part of the group. He guaranteed good likenesses of both of us. Another of Lois' dazzling feats of imagination! If he agrees to do a job of work for charity, absolutely free of charge, he always intends to have his own way about it. And if he only has crazy ideas in his head he can't help that. After all he's an artist and has a better right than other people to make a fool of himself.

"Do you seriously suggest I'm going to squeeze myself into all that grocery-tin armor?" I demanded, when he had finished.

"No, you won't have to do that. All I want to do is to study the two attitudes, those of horse and rider."

"Well, the Majestic One's not going to hold up his forepaws with the Hungarian and me both on his back together. He's not quite such an acrobat as all that. You'll have to get a dray horse, and a whopper at that!"

"Not a bit of it!" Lois retorted. "He'll easily be able to manage the Countess as well. She's only a flyweight!"

The Hungarian said she believed he was right.

"Yes, but look here, he won't be able to balance on his hind legs for hours on end, till Lois has finished hammering his blocks together!"

"He won't have to. I'll simply take a few photographs and then carve from them," Lois said.

"Well then, why not just enlarge a photograph and hang it up on the church wall? You'll save yourself a lot of work and you'll be able to use all that nice wood to better purpose, when winter comes, in the stove!" I told him.

I was still not particularly taken with the idea of the Majestic One sweating his hide off with two people up, simply for the sake of making an appearance in church as a horse of sacred character. What good would that do him? He would go to the horses' heaven in any case, as he had never murdered, stolen, lied, betrayed, or committed any other human misdeeds in his life. All he had done was to graze the rockery bare. And that was only because he was hungry. And he did once give me a bad spill, so that the Hungarian thought I was done for. But that was absolutely all. Lois really ought to let him off, and me into the bargain. That would be pulling a fast one, to make a man with my nickname kill dragons and protect widows and orphans in the guise of Saint George! The Hungarian, however, was in favor, she said, of doing something for her soul's salvation while she had the chance.

"Right-ho, then. You do it by yourself, Hungarian," I said. "You can go and be a saint on your own. But we two others, the Majestic One and I, are not going to take part in any such nonsense. We don't want to run into trouble with the episcopal authorities in Salzburg. I'm not keen on officials of any kind, earthly or heavenly. Once you get into their hands, you pay through the nose for it!"

The Hungarian ended up by calling me an ass, which she seemed to think would make me give in. But I had another objection. My ankle! What a bit of luck it was for me that something had gone wrong with it!

I pointed out, accordingly, that I was only a miserable cripple, incapable of mounting a horse. But the Hungarian retorted that it would be the doctor's business to decide whether I could be made fit enough to fight dragons. Consequently, we would go over to Salzburg, so that the doctor could take the plaster off and see how I was getting on.

All she needed to do now was to mention that *capriole* I had mendaciously referred to in my telegram as a heroic deed which had come to grief. That would have finished me up altogether. For the Majestic One had never been able to manage a *capriole* in his life.

When Lois heard the Hungarian disposing of me in this fashion he walked off tranquilly, with the air of a man satisfied that his plans are well under way. I felt furious at the idea that he might be thinking I was merely the Hungarian's gigolo. I told her so, too. She answered at once that I could have my own way if I liked, in which case the beautiful statue would never be made at all. She didn't care for gigolos, for carpet-knights, she said. But she uttered those self-sacrificing words with the expression of a child whose chocolate has fallen in the horse dung. I felt so sorry for her that I there and then agreed to the whole show.

"Right," she rejoined. "Then we go ahead with the sacred monument. But, remember, it's only because you have expressly ordered it, of your own free will!"

That made the whole thing clear, of course. The position was that against my will I had demanded, with all the forcibility I could muster, that the group should be executed. For that to make sense I should have to be Saint George himself in person.

That afternoon we drove over to Salzburg to see the doctor. The Hungarian told him, straight away, that she had nursed me as carefully as if I had been a sick horse and that she had insisted again and again that I was not to move my leg.

After this, it would have been discourteous of the doctor to have said anything except that he was immeasurably delighted with the progress my ankle had made and that there was no longer any need for plaster. An elastic bandage only would be necessary. But I should still have to take care of that leg, he said, as it couldn't yet bear my weight, owing to its weakness. He told me, however, to flex the joint as much as possible, to prevent its stiffening.

"Can he ride, then?" the Hungarian asked. At once the doctor, as if he had been simply waiting for his cue, exclaimed heartily:

"Riding would be excellent for it! The movements made by the ankle in the stirrup are the very thing he needs!"

I could have poisoned the fellow. The cunning old pill merchant had repeated word for word what the Hungarian said, as if he had had his palms greased for him!

"Aren't you glad you can ride again now?" she asked me on the drive home.

"Yes, I shall enjoy riding all right. But as for making a monkey of myself in that silly group, for which I'm not in the least suited, I can't stand the idea!"

"Well, now you've made your bed you'll just have to lie on it," observed the Hungarian solemnly, as if I had already faithfully promised Lois to cooperate.

"By the way, Unholy George," she added after a while, "you will show me, won't you, that *capriole* the Majestic One is practicing just now?"

I had been afraid that was going to be the next move. The Hungarian's memory is as good as a horse's.

"I shall need a little more time first. Otherwise I shall probably get another spill and smash up my leg again."

"Oh, of course, Unholy George. You'll have to get properly fit again before you show me," she replied. But her voice sounded as though she doubted whether the Majestic One and I would ever manage a *capriole*, even if we kept on trying till Judgment Day. She might be quite right to think so. It was what I myself also feared, with good reason. The Majestic One did not take naturally to the *capriole*. He had become a champion at the *levade*. He could also manage two or three *courbettes*, leaping forward on his hind legs without his forelegs touching the ground. "He hops like a kangaroo," the priest had once remarked when he was looking on. But that man's entirely ignorant of *haute école* riding. He ought to stick to his breviary.

When we reached home I scrambled out of the Gentian without assistance. I found my ankle frightfully weak. But for that very reason I felt all the keener to have a shot at riding. I still couldn't pull a boot on over the bandage, so I decided to ride just as I was, in my buckskin shorts and stockings.

No one ever saddled a horse so quickly as the Hungarian did on that occasion. The Majestic One neighed as soon as I had mounted. My ankle pained me in the stirrup, so I slung them over and rode without, in the true *haute école* style. Aha, I thought, we can still put up a good show, the Majestic One and I! We performed a *levade* in the ring such as only we two were capable of. I felt as though it was only now that I had started living again properly. When one's spirits rise like that, one is always prone to take chances. So I tried to make the Majestic One take a leap out of the *piaffe*. As soon as I tapped his quarters with the switch he let fly all right. But his forelegs remained on the ground, as if his hoofs had been made of lead. The result was a perfect *capriole* in the standing posture. The French Riding School at Saumur would have called it a work of art.

"No good!" I cried to the Hungarian, as the leap miscarried. "I still haven't got the guts!"

Even as I spoke I felt like a brute for trying to force a *capriole* on the Majestic One, though he had never been able to do one and never shown any desire to. It was pretty much the same as if someone had wanted me to talk Chinese. I just couldn't. But, because I had told that lie, he would have to suffer as well as myself. Any close friendship is liable to involve that sort of thing.

That evening we resumed the tale of the Majestic One's youth and of the period in which we ourselves, in our own affair, showed an inexperience in love over which we could now only shake our heads.

"Well, Hungarian," I started off. "We're not done with the tragic part yet. It really only begins properly now!"

"I know. We were given the works, weren't we? But go ahead. Let's get the whole chapter of accidents over quick!"

"Stand by, then," I said, making a fresh start. "Three days after I had been made to sit on your bed a frost descended on the spring night of my young love, which had by then come to resemble an untouched flower on an alpine pasture——"

She interrupted me again.

"You can read the tosh people write any time you like, Unholy George. But the stilted drivel you're talking now is enough to make anyone shudder! I don't like it, let me tell you!"

"All right then! I'll just blurt it all out as it comes! I don't give a damn for that high-falutin style!"

"On you go then! It can't be any worse than it is already!"

"Well, so our love was platonic, as they call it," I continued, more bluntly. "It had to be. It wasn't because we had the souls of angels. Then misfortune came thick and fast. My money ran out. I had been poverty-stricken enough before then. No one could make a decent living out of riding in those days. I had had a wretched time of it in our lovely Vienna. The staff at the Spanish Riding School had been obliged to find consolation in their art for their lean living conditions.

"I had already been staying at Reserl's inn on credit for

three days. I didn't like to tell you I was broke and couldn't do anything but ride a horse.

"At last a letter came from Leopold in Vienna. He wrote that I was to take over two horses immediately. Pay would be at the rate of a hundred schillings a month for each animal. If you haven't got any money, you have to do anything anyone says and even take on jobs you don't like. I already knew what it meant to break in horses for people who flit round the Prater, sweating off their superfluous fat or simply to let others see them.

"So I gradually broke the news to you that I should have to leave. You became depressed, probably thinking that some woman had written to me from Vienna. Leopold writes such a delicate hand that it might easily be taken for a feminine one. And as I wasn't going to let you get away with that idea at any price I told you everything. I said that one simply had to earn money, times were so bad and the horseman's spirit a mere shadow of its former self. I added that I must leave for Vienna at once in case someone else got the horses first. You saw my point but said, nevertheless, that I was only to stay away a couple of days at most.

"I objected that I had pressing debts to settle. But you replied that it was a long time since you yourself had bothered about such things and that your own debts came to as much as a staff officer's in peacetime. But there's a certain difference between a Countess having debts of ten thousand pengos on her estate and a poor devil of a demobilized lieutenant owing ten schillings at an inn. So I stuck to my decision and begged you either to come with me to Vienna or follow me there a few days later. But you didn't want to. When I said you ought to do so for my sake, you answered that it was for both our sakes that you were unwilling to. I must confess, Hungarian, that I never understood what you meant. Even today I can't see why you had to make us both suffer so in order to preserve our love."

"I'll tell you why it was, Unholy George," said the Hungarian, as she took my hands. "You've often thought you understood me and yet you've completely missed the point. I've never once been angry with you for that reason, even when it wasn't easy to keep my temper. You know, things had been happening to us pretty fast at that time. You weren't the first man I had been fond of, nor was I your first love. It all started like a game. But a fragrance eventually reached it which came from the pastures, right up there into the guest room. We had found ourselves so very close to the good earth and to each other in our affection for the little Majestic One, who had enabled our hands to meet in his bristly foal's hair. And my own wishes appeared so natural to me that I was ready to listen to you. In the morning we should have woken up close to each other on that narrow, creaking bedstead. Down below in the inn yard the cock would have proclaimed the new day. Your arm would have been round me and at first I should have wondered, with amazement, what sort of a man I had fallen in love with. Stubble would have grown on your chin during the night and at the first glance I should hardly have recognized you. That was the sort of morning, Unholy George, that we should have had after our first night in the little guest room. Then we should have heard the horses going out into the pasture and after that we shouldn't have waited long. Out we should have gone into the pastures to the horses and the little Majestic One, to thank him for giving us so much happiness. And what would it have been like in Vienna later on? The hotel porter, naturally, would assign a room with a double bed to the lady and gentleman. And that Saint George of mine would write in the register that he was with his wife. He would put on such an innocent air that the porter would realize instantly what the position was. In the morning the street noises would have woken us. Well, you know, I didn't want it that way. But you remember, of course, what actually did happen in the end, not in Vienna, but in Budapest. I didn't want you to come to my room there. But the gypsy music was still echoing in my blood and I thought you would be hurt if I left you standing outside the locked door. Afterward you were so discreet as to be positively stupid, Unholy George. I never thought I could go on loving you. But the very next day we were out on the Puszta among the horses and that night I realized that I was going to love Unholy George for the rest of my life. I could look up at the stars and see what eternity meant. And I felt that time and eternity had become one. You know, Unholy George, in our closest intimacy we too became one in feeling. I can never be grateful enough to you for that!"

I remained silent. After a while she added: "I made us lose each other for three years, because I didn't come with you to Vienna at that time. How I had to suffer for it! Those three years were filled with longing for you. I could never find another man like you, Unholy George, with so many shortcomings and yet so tender and so selfish, as only a man in love can be. Well, you go on with the story now."

"Yes, that parting was an unpleasant experience, Hungarian. As you didn't want to cry, you took up a hard and cold attitude, which made me think all was over between us. I asked whether we should meet again in Vienna in the Spanish Riding School. Possibly, you said. I was dreadfully afraid you wouldn't come. I added that you would only have to ask Leopold where I was. I wanted to give you my address. But you only answered, with a cold stare, 'Once I start looking for you I shall find you all right. Bye-bye, Saint George! Good riding!'

"I couldn't move. I stood there in front of you in the inn yard, my suitcase in my hand. I couldn't believe it was all going to end like this. It seemed impossible that anything that had begun with such gentle affection could be so rudely shattered.

"I asked timidly, 'Won't you come a bit of the way with me?'

"You shook your head. You knew that if you said another word the tears would begin to flow. So I turned away, to prevent your seeing that I myself was now in the grip of such misery that I could have wailed aloud. Then I left. I didn't even take a last look round, except at the pasture, where the Majestic One, separated from his mother, was standing among the other foals, as lonely as myself. I ducked under the wire and called him. He came to me at once and let me put my arm round his neck.

" 'Listen, Majestic One,' I whispered, 'we shall have to do our best to get along alone now. You have no mother now and I have lost the woman you love as much as I do. If I could take you with me, it would be some consolation.

But I'm only a poor helpless creature like you. I could never be any real use to you, for I haven't even got enough for myself, so there's no question of my being able to put anything in the manger for you. You'd have a rotten time of it with me and you'd better stay where you are. You'll be a fine fellow one of these days, the sort to take people's breath away when you come to show what you can do in the Spanish Riding School. You'll meet me again there. You may recognize me or you may not. Don't worry about that, Majestic One. Nothing matters to me now. I've only the past to think of. There isn't any future for me. If the Hungarian Countess ever comes to see you, be as good-tempered and cheerful with her as you always were, so that she'll see I'm not angry with her. Off with you now, Majestic One! Misfortune's infectious. It's like a disease. Run! Or you'll catch it, too!'

"I gave him a slap on the hindquarters. It startled him so much that he leaped away from me. Then I crawled back through the fence on to the road.

"The Majestic One neighed after me twice. Every now and then I stood still and waved back at him. Perhaps it might be a good omen, I thought, that farewell neighing from a horse. But I realized that by the next day he would have already forgotten me, in his games with his little girl friend Deflorata. He had stopped back-lipping with her now and ran races with her instead. Like all foals he would then develop a passion for gnawing bark and soon, too, he would be going out into the pasture with the other little stallions, separated from the fillies. There he would find a world of wonders, with a new experience for him every day, finer and better ones than any human being could provide.

"Well, when I got to Vienna, Leopold hardly recognized me. He asked what had been happening to me. But I didn't answer. I just got on with my work, training those two horses. They belonged to people who a few months before had never dreamed of riding. I now had to teach them. They were a mother and daughter. The esteemed father, not so long ago, had been driving a coal cart, with a half-starved old crock in the shafts. He had himself driven in a motor car now and kept trying to start intimate conversations with me about horses. The old woman was as up and coming as the young one, who was not so bad-looking and learned fairly quickly. But rather than go to bed with them I preferred to hand the horses over to someone else, who made up for his inadequate understanding of horses by knowing a good deal more about females.

"I denied myself every relaxation at that time. I saved up all the money I could spare. Leopold sometimes took me along to drink new wine in the vineyards and on one of those occasions I mentioned the Hungarian Countess' name to him. He knew it well and told me that her father had been shot during the Revolution. The family had lost everything. The daughter only inherited her father's passion for horses. It did me good to be able to talk about you, Hungarian. After we had got home I told Leopold I should like to take the money I had saved and return to Piber. I said you must be there now, for a year had passed and May had come round again, and——"

At this point the Hungarian interrupted me.

"Listen, Unholy George, I'm awfully tired. Let's go up-stairs. I'm so glad to be here with you. It's been a great bit of luck that everything did turn out so well for us three. Today I want to enjoy that feeling of being quite sure that you are mine. You must let me go to sleep at your side, and in your arms, so that I can keep warm!"

9

The priest did actually let us have the book in which it was stated that, though Mohammed had written favorably of horses in the Koran, he was reluctant to trust himself to them and consequently really preferred asses and camels. The priest handed me the book with his thumb already marking the place. But I put it aside at the time. I didn't want to read about such disgraceful revelations concerning the prophet while the priest was there.

After he had gone I glanced through the pages. It was a worm-eaten old volume, dealing only with horses, the kind of book it was difficult to imagine any priest but our own possessing. It was very good stuff, though. There were a lot of pithy sayings in it. One of them read:

> *"Who takes no joy in a falchion bright*
> *Or in a proud steed no delight,*
> *Or a buxom lass loves not to see,*
> *Hath never a heart in his whole body!"*

"I say, Hungarian," I called out. "Just look at this! The very motto for our front door!"

She came over and read the verse, thought it magnificent. Another one followed, which ran:

> *"Our earthly paradise,*
> *On the back of a horse it lies.*
> *In the body's health we find it too,*
> *And in a woman's heart so true!"*

That, too, the Hungarian considered, might pass muster. But as we had only one front door it seemed to me that the Majestic One ought also to have a motto, for the door of his stable. It might be either of the two stanzas. Lois could paint the letters on the right kind of wood in gay, variegated colors that would stand weathering. It was the least he could do to compensate me for posing as a model for Saint George.

Accordingly, I whistled from the window on two fingers. The whole village immediately buzzed with the news that Lois and Unholy George had once more got their heads together and were hatching a plot. Lois had a sound reason for doing me a good turn. He came over straight away and I told him exactly what I wanted him to do.

As the Hungarian was busy in the kitchen, I was able at

the same time to tell Lois, in a whisper, about something else I wanted, which was to be a secret.

"Read that," I said. "You're to paint that for the living room."

Lois read out, with a grin:

"Three things in this world can kick, I'll own,
They're women, wine and a horse half grown!"

Then we got into the thick of the really well-peppered stuff. The reader was warned to beware of three things: the frontage of a female, the hindquarters of a horse, and the aspect of a flatterer in every direction.

"I say, that'ud make a good motto for Farmer Schwaiger," exclaimed Lois. "His old woman's just been leathering him for never leaving the skivvy alone. And that Noric Alps mare of his, which had taken a dislike to him, passed him such a smasher at the smith's the other day that his nose nearly went through the back of his head. He also lost about a thousand schillings over that mineral spring racket, simply because they told him that when the spa was put up he'd be made general manager. I tell you what, I'll write out that motto and then we'll go and stick it up on his house at night."

I was in on that, as anyone who knows me can tell you. We also found another motto, which would do beautifully for the bedroom here at home, where the furniture was all a bit sketchy.

"I'll put that one up for you, too," said Lois.

"Not a word to the Hungarian," I murmured. For just then she came in, looking us over as if we had been a couple of kids on the point of climbing an apple tree, but now pretending to be the most innocent creatures in the world.

She didn't stay long, though.

"Put that book of the priest's into cold storage," said Lois. "Behave as though you'd forgotten all about it. But isn't it a bit queer he should have such red-hot stuff in his library?"

"My word, he let himself in for something with his Mohammed!" I exclaimed exultantly. "That soon showed us what sort of books he reads when no one's looking! Imagine it! Our priest himself, eh?"

"You must let me have it, so that I can copy out the mottoes," Lois said. I made him promise, though, before I let him go, to take the greatest care of that precious volume.

"I'll have it all ready by tomorrow," he told me. "Cheerio!"

After he had gone my conscience did rather prick me about the motto I had chosen for the bedroom. But I didn't think the Hungarian would raise any objection. After all, the thing was from a popular ballad and out of a book belonging to the priest into the bargain.

I had just come to that point in my reflections when I saw the priest turning in at the garden gate. I guessed right. He had come for the book. Apparently it had occurred to him that he ought not to let it out of his clutches.

"But I should like to read it all through, Father," I told him. "Let me keep it a few days longer."

"Well, I don't mind your reading it. But don't let the Countess see it, whatever you do!" he exclaimed, with considerable excitement.

"You're quite right, Father," I answered. "I was just glancing through it to begin with and I found some of the mottoes were so highly flavored that I locked it up straight away. That Hungarian Countess of mine has awfully refined feelings, you know!"

The Hungarian came out of the kitchen at that moment and asked the priest to what we owed the pleasure of this further visit of his. As the honest man of God seemed quite at a loss to hit upon a credible lie without delay I answered for him.

"He's just been telling me in strict confidence that he'd love another drop of that Hungarian wine. It gives him such a good appetite for lunch."

The Hungarian considered this request such an honor that she at once rushed off and fetched a bottle of wine. She was back again so quickly that the priest hadn't time to think of any objection.

We made ourselves so snug round the table together that on such a fine morning it seemed positively sinful. The Hungarian kept one ear cocked in the direction of the kitchen, because that day we were going to have Hungarian goulash with spaghetti. But she did not leave the table until the priest rose. He managed it at the second attempt. The Hungarian and I had drunk two glasses. He had polished off the rest.

"God bless you both!" said he. We replied that it had been a pleasure.

But, heavens above! Once he got out into the hot sunlight he went under. He wavered as though he were following a winding mountain path instead of our straight-cut village lane.

The Hungarian said we shouldn't have done it.

"But, hang it all! If he gulps down wine as if it were water, it's his own fault!"

Later on, as we were sitting over our goulash, the priest's housekeeper, old Emerentia, came in, terribly upset.

"What on earth's happened to our good Father? He came home, wouldn't eat anything, and flopped down there and then on the leather couch in his study. I asked what was wrong. He muttered something rude about Saint George and then started talking Latin. It suddenly came to me that he must have meant Unholy George——"

"What was it he said in Latin?" I asked her.

"H'm—let's see—yes, there was something about Culpa and Maximilian. But I'm sure he's not a saint!"

"Wasn't it *mea culpa, mea maxima culpa*?" I asked.

"So it was, that's dead right!" Emerentia said.

"You see!" I said to the Hungarian. "He realizes himself that it's his own fault if he boozes like a camel in an oasis!"

Emerentia went for me tooth and nail for that. She said her priest was not a boozer and that she'd report me to the bishop's office in Salzburg for my loose tongue. She whirled off in a rage. The Hungarian gave me such a stiff lecture that I felt as though it was I myself and not the priest who had got so easily fuddled.

But as I didn't say a word in my own defense she soon shut up of her own accord. She probably thought that remorse had made me dumb and consequently felt sorry for me.

She was the first to smile. But I went on looking serious

and remorseful until she told me in earnest that it was time I laughed again.

"I was laughing all the time," I said. "I laughed so much, right down inside me, that I ached all over!"

She told me, in reply, that I was a hopeless case and that was all there was to it.

Nevertheless, I insisted on continuing the subject.

"I say, Hungarian, I wonder if the priest will go off to Salzburg tomorrow and confess that he got boiled?"

"I don't think so," the Hungarian said in an extremely doubtful tone. "He can forgive himself his own sins, can't he?"

"Lucky devil! When I consider my own case, now——"

"Your conscience doesn't trouble you in the very slightest," she interrupted, finishing the sentence for me.

"Well, that's why I'm called Unholy George, isn't it?"

"Oh, you can always back out of anything," she retorted grimly. "Go and lie down now. Sleep off your wickedness!"

"I can't go to sleep without a kiss."

"Stay awake, then!"

She started clearing away. I lay down on the settee by the window. When she returned to the room I pretended to be asleep, making my breathing sound quite regular. I heard her come over to me. Then, suddenly, I felt a kiss on my lips. Like lightning, I seized her in my arms and didn't let her go till the kiss had taken her breath away.

As I released her, I groaned longingly, in a most realistic fashion, and muttered sleepily, "What a lovely dream that was!"

The Hungarian's eyes opened wide. She wasn't quite sure whether I was pulling her leg or not. The fact is that

I do extraordinary things when I'm dreaming. Once I woke the Hungarian up in the pitch dark and asked her the price of a cartload of dung. As she couldn't tell me right away I turned round and went off to sleep again. Meanwhile she sat up in bed till daybreak, trying to work out exactly what the cost might be, for she had become quite interested, herself, in the question. The next morning I had no idea what had been worrying me in my dream and we were at sixes and sevens until breakfast time because the Hungarian hadn't had a proper night's rest.

Another time I actually started using my fists in my sleep and gave her a smart tap right on the nose. She has a pretty little nose. One might more accurately describe it as a noselet. Nevertheless, I scored a bull's-eye on it in my dream. I didn't wake up properly until I heard her crying. And that was all I knew about it, except that I had dreamed I was arguing with Lois and couldn't convince him.

"Oh, so you meant it for him?" the Hungarian had inquired. At that time we were living on her estate in Hungary. A few months later we returned to my place and Lois called to welcome us home. She immediately gave him one on the nose and told him it was from me, she was merely passing it on.

Lois stared like a goose in a thunderstorm. As soon as I had explained matters he wanted to start a roughhouse with me, as he always retaliates when anybody hits him.

"Look here," the Hungarian said, "don't start those excited dreams of yours again with me, or I shall go and stay at the priest's!"

"Come and lie down here and console me," I said.

"What, at that open window?"

"Well, shut it then. And you can fasten the shutters, too!"

But she wouldn't, because there would be gossip in the village whether one had the window open or shut.

That day, however, the sleeping problem was solved in quite a different way.

We suddenly heard a loud neighing outside. We jumped up and saw the Majestic One make a tremendous leap over the fence into the front garden.

"Damn and blast!" I cried. "That's the vet's mare again!" She was being driven past in the cart belonging to Wastl, Mödlinger's farm hand, and had come to a halt. She didn't want to go on. She wanted to join the Majestic One.

"Hey, Wastl! What are you up to?" I shouted.

"I've got to take her to the smith, the bitch! She's lost a shoe. The doctor's at our place, because our sow's got the red murrain!"

While he was talking the mare had broken loose and the Majestic One was dancing round her on his hind legs. They were both squealing as if they wanted to invite the whole village to their wedding. Wastl made his escape, as he didn't want to be knocked out. We two looked on, without making any attempt to bring the Majestic One to reason. There was no point in preventing him from offering the pretty young mare proof of his affection.

Everyone who was at home and not out in the fields came running up. Soon the whole village had arrived. And yet they're always complaining to us that the day's too short for them to get their work done!

Lois and Mirl, of course, also turned up. Our respected priest alone continued to sleep off his liquor, without hearing or seeing the slightest thing.

The vet arrived at full speed with his whip, like an avenging angel. But he was too late. Nevertheless, he tried to intervene. But he had reckoned without Lois, who seized the whip and broke the stock twice across his knee.

"No one's going to beat a horse outside our place!" he yelled at the vet.

The latter bawled back that the horse was his own property. But immediately the whole of the assembled village took up a hostile attitude toward the cattle medico.

He ought to have been pleased at getting a good foal for nothing, they told him. And if he ill-treated that mare they swore they'd send for the other vet, the young fellow. As soon as he saw that the ax was being laid to the tree of his livelihood he roared at Wastl to get moving and take the mare on to the smith. But the latter was himself present and led the horse away there and then. The Kladruber was quite willing to go with him, for the smith slapped her neck and talked soothingly to her. The Majestic One stood by as if he had been carved out of wood, wondering what on earth all the fuss was about, when all he had done was to follow his natural instincts.

He uttered one farewell neigh to his mare. Then he wheeled and made straight for the vet, who instantly took to flight. The Majestic One bounded after him for a short distance. Then he trotted back alongside the fence. The villagers shook with laughter. So did we, as we watched from the window.

I called him and he did look across at me. But he wasn't

going to bother to jump back over the hedge. Lois had to open the gate for him.

"Wonderful what a horse like that can do when he's in love!" said I to the Hungarian.

She replied that people were just the same, the only thing was, they always regretted it afterward. She gave me such a meaning look as she spoke that it practically amounted to an affectionate rebuke.

"You're both tarred with the same brush, you and your Majestic One!"

The stallion came up to us at the window and pushed his velvety muzzle into the Hungarian's face, as he always does to show his liking for anyone. She ran off immediately to fetch him a lump of sugar.

"I have to be nice to you two ruffians, I suppose," she said. With that our triple alliance had a single heart and soul again.

That evening I was just thinking that I might perhaps evade the storytelling today, when the Hungarian reminded me of my duty. She had been as patient as a lamb with me throughout the day. So I lit a Virginia cigar with great formality, made myself comfortable in the armchair, and began at the precise point in the tale where we had left off.

"Well then, when I got back to Piber you were not there. Reserl, at the inn, asked me for news of you, for she had quite taken you to her heart. But I had heard nothing from you. All I had was a photograph showing you standing in front of a herd of yearling fillies with your back turned to the spectator.

"When I got upstairs into the guest room I felt ready to die of misery. The place had a wooden sort of look, like a mere dormitory, only endurable in the dark. I just put down my suitcase and bolted downstairs again. Reserl buttonholed me once more. I mustn't tell her stories, she said. She was sure you would be coming along, too. I gave her a positively rude answer and rushed out to see the yearling stallions.

"I recognized the Majestic One instantly. But he had forgotten me. He had grown much lighter in color. The snow-white hair was already showing through his dark hide. He had come to the years of indiscretion, too, forever tussling and romping with his comrades like a mad thing.

"He was grazing quietly among the other horses when he suddenly threw up his head and in a moment had nipped one of his companions in the neck. The other reared and retaliated. Both stood stiffly on their hind legs and lashed away at each other with their forefeet. A third joined in the fight, attacking the Majestic One. Then all the rest stopped grazing. They scattered, racing across the pasture at a wild gallop. Tufts of grass flew up from the soft earth under their hoofs. But as suddenly as the hurricane had come on, it died down. The stallions bounded on for a short distance. Then they peacefully dropped their muzzles to the grass again and went on grazing.

"I stayed a fortnight. Just as the Majestic One was beginning to renew our former cordial friendship I had to leave once more, as my money had run out again.

"There's not much more to tell. I had a bad time of it, working for a while on commission, then as racing correspondent on a newspaper. But I left that job when I found that dirty work had been going on. One of the horses had been doped. I was able to prove the fact in court. But the case went against me, nevertheless. The owner of the horse was a brother-in-law of the publisher of the paper. If ever I got any money I used to hire any poor devil of a horse from Tattersall and ride him round the Prater at a walk, or else dismount and let him graze, so that he, too, might for once in his life get something out of it. I kept thinking of you, Hungarian, at that time and was always looking at that photograph of you from the back. I couldn't help thinking of the Majestic One either, for you two had become, after all, the only creatures in the world that I cared about. If a woman and a horse are both tugging at your heart, no wonder it grows weak. But I couldn't allow myself to weaken. I had to keep my head above water in the whirlpool of that crazy gamble for money, in which a man might still be rich one day and the next a beggar. I hate talking about it, Hungarian. Thank goodness, I've forgotten most of it now. Whenever I could I took refuge in the Spanish Riding School. I found more consolation there than I should have done in frequenting the Church of St. Michael. The spirit prevailing in the Spanish School was healthy, a true horseman's spirit, that had nothing in common with the demoniac one that reigned outside. I always felt safe in the Spanish School. Whenever I left it I invariably regained my faith that the spirit of the horseman would return to the whole city of Vienna. I was right. That was just what did happen. The bad times passed away like an illness and even my own prospects improved. Leopold managed to get me a job as stable manager in a riding establishment, which put me in touch with horses once more.

"But I didn't stay there long. Two years had now passed.

I visited Piber again, in the wild hope that you might be there, simply because May had come round for the second time. But once more I had to wander about the pastures alone and the Majestic One seemed to regard me as a total stranger. He was quite white now except for a few shadowy patches in his hide. He far exceeded the rest in strength and grace. He was still fond of romping. But whenever the herd dashed off at a gallop he was invariably a few lengths ahead. Reserl, who had a memory like a horse's, pestered me again for news of you. She wanted to know whether I had at least written to you. But you had told me three years before that you would soon find me once you started looking for me. I didn't want to come to you, and I didn't like to write, without being asked . . ."

"All the same, you would have been welcome, Unholy George," said the Hungarian. "My father had been shot during the Revolution. The estate had been plundered. The herds had been driven off. I had to build everything up again from scratch. But the year I visited Piber, thinking that we should soon be doing well, as the fields were in good shape and small herds of my own were again grazing in the Puszta, my stables burned down. I lost all my cattle and horses owing to hoof-and-mouth disease. The banks that had been lending me money threatened to sell me up. I almost gave up hope at that time. I went round Budapest cadging for credit. You can imagine the interest some people wanted to charge me. At home I had to run the whole place on my own. My staff had left. Only Janos, who had looked after my father's horses, stuck to me. With his help and God's I managed to establish a small herd of horses again on the Puszta, with Janos as Cszikos.* If you had only come along at that time, Unholy George! I couldn't very well write and invite you, for I had sent you away and I couldn't bear to summon you after that, to help me out of my difficulties. Whenever I thought of you, I always felt that I owed you something. And then I still had to keep my promise that you were to have your Majestic One. I pulled all the wires I could at the Ministry in Budapest to enlist their help in enabling me to buy the Majestic One in Piber. Fortunately the position in Vienna at that time was such that they preferred cash in the till to a young stallion at grass. You go on with the story now and say what faces you made when you found that the Majestic One was to leave!"

"It all happened the very next day. The evening before, the stud manager had told me that the Majestic One had been sold. He said the buyer was a Hungarian Countess. I dashed down to the stud headquarters at the Castle and after some wangling found that it was you who had bought him. He was to be put on the train at Koflach early the next morning.

"I racked my brains all the rest of that day. I believed you were now going to take away all I had left, the last thing I had, though it wasn't really my own. But I meant to see you just once more and tell you it wasn't fair. But I had no idea how I was going to get at you. I had only just enough money to pay my keep at Piber and my fare back to Vienna. While I was playing a game of billiards that night with the director of the stud, I asked him in a casual

---

* *Cszikos:* an expert horseman in charge of a group of privately owned horses on the Puszta. *Cf.* the Argentine *Gaucho*.

way who would be going with the stallion. He growled out something to the effect that it was all he could do to manage with his staff, so many of them were leaving, and now there was this transport to arrange as well. So I told him that he knew me all right and could trust me. Of course he could, he said. Then I made a clean breast of it. I said I would be willing to take the stallion to Hungary for the same money as he would otherwise be paying a groom. He didn't take long to think it over. He agreed, thanked me for doing him a good turn, and said he would be responsible to the Ministry of Agriculture for the action taken. He added that he knew you and I were acquainted and considered, accordingly, that the affair would be in good hands if I took charge of it.

"I didn't sleep much that night. I could hardly wait for morning to come, so that I could march off with the Majestic One at the end of a halter, to take him to the station at Koflach. Twice I had left Piber alone and now I was going to have the Majestic One for company! I should be able to groom him during the long journey and sleep with him in the truck.

"The station master told me that the journey would take three days. Only three days! Then I would have to say good-by to the Majestic One for ever! I should then have only Deflorata, his little girl friend, left. I remembered seeing her at her graceful play in the pasture with the other fillies.

"I made the Majestic One as comfortable as I could in the horse truck. We had plenty of straw and kept the sliding door open, with a breast-high wooden trellis as a guard. We were thus able to look out of the truck and breathe fresh air. I let the stallion loose, though the station master had said that I ought to tie him up. But the fellow didn't know what he was talking about. We had to wait an hour before we could be coupled to the goods train. After Graz we should be going on with a passenger train. At Graz I was able to walk the Majestic One up and down outside, so that he could have some exercise. We had another long wait for the train. It was not until nightfall that we crossed the frontier at Steinamanger. When the Hungarian officials came to examine my passport we found we knew one another. Consequently, customs formalities were brief. They were all too brief for me. For the guard said that, because of the horse, the truck would be sent with the express to Budapest, so that we could reach Kecskemét in the afternoon.

"I was very glad, for the Majestic One's sake, that the journey would be a short one. But I was losing a day, myself. He behaved very well and gave no trouble on the way. He had got quite used to me. We had made friends now for the third time. The night was rather chilly and I lay down close to him in the straw to keep myself warm. He woke me discreetly in the morning, nudging my shoulder to make me do my duty by grooming, feeding, and watering him.

"At Budapest we did not change trains. We only had to stay in the truck while we were shunted. Exactly two hours later the truck was uncoupled from the express at Kecskemét. Janos was waiting for us at the station with the light carriage and pair. He could speak German and complimented me on the good condition of the stallion. He said the Countess would be very pleased. I pumped him a bit for news of you. He talked of you as if you had been a saint. He told me how hard the times had been and how, nevertheless, you had pulled through. The Majestic One's halter was tied to the back of the carriage and he trotted along behind us at a good round pace, glad to be able to use his legs at last.

"As it would take us over an hour to reach the Bugac district of the Puszta, we kept to a steady gait, so that the Majestic One could arrive with a dry hide.

"Janos said he did not know precisely why the Countess had bought the Lipizzaner stallion. He only knew that she had constantly spoken of him, saying that by this time he must have grown into a regal horse, if he had fulfilled his promise as a foal. I felt very curious as to whether you had also discussed me with Janos. But I did not like to ask, as I was not at all sure what your attitude to me might be after such a long time. Did I know the stud at Piber, Janos inquired. And did I know a certain man there—Janos had never heard his name—to whom the Countess had referred merely as a lieutenant who knew a lot about horses and rode well.

" 'Oh yes, that chap,' I answered. 'Of course I know him, Janos. He's not quite such a tremendous fellow as the Countess seems to think. But she's not far wrong!'

"Janos observed, unexpectedly, that a man was badly needed on the estate. He grinned at me as he spoke, as if he knew more than he was letting on. He added that the stud had sent a wire.

" 'Good lord!' I burst out. 'Then you must know who I am——'

" 'Sure, we know, lieutenant!' Janos said. He gave such a roar of laughter that the horses in front broke into a gallop. The springless carriage bumped and jolted over the pitted, grass-grown steppe. Janos cracked his whip, shouting that the Countess would be pleased, ay, that she would!

"I seized him by the shoulder.

" 'She'll be pleased, Janos, you say?' I yelled at him.

" 'Ay, lieutenant! My lady the Countess, she's pleased all right!' he bawled back at me.

"We pulled up close beside a herd of horses that were being watered at a draw-well. Janos alighted, giving me the reins and the whip. He untied the Majestic One from the back of the carriage and placed him in front, beside the offside horse.

"Between the trees, which never stand close together on the Puszta, we could see the gleaming white buildings of the estate. I was to drive on, Janos said. He would have to stay with the horses, to see that the young herdsman did his job properly.

"I set the horses a good pace. Janos yelled encouragement after me. The carriage lumbered over the irregularities in the ground, sending me high into the air from the driving seat. Ahead, the two Puszta horses were galloping and with them went the Majestic One, his mane flying and his tail streaming. The way to the estate seemed endless. I cracked the whip to make the pace as fast as the harness would stand. I had to brace my feet hard against the splashboard. My hat flew off, away into the Puszta. A lot I cared about a hat! To hell with it! On to the estate, that was all I wanted, and to lose no time over it!

"At last I could see the gate. It was standing open. We dashed through it into the courtyard. The hoofs clattered loudly on the paving. The two carriage horses pranced as

I reined them in and the Majestic One reared recklessly, neighing.

"I jumped down and unharnessed him. Then I took him to the foot of the staircase leading to the veranda of the residence. You came down the steps, dressed in your national costume and carrying white bread and a glass of wine.

"The whole thing was so solemn and ceremonious that I got a lump in my throat and tears rose to my eyes.

" 'Welcome, Saint George,' you said. 'Eat and drink!'

"I took the loaf, broke a piece off, and raised it to my lips. But all I could do was to chew it. It wouldn't go down. So I took the glass and drank, holding the Majestic One's rein under my arm. While I was drinking he ate the piece of bread in my hand. As soon as I had gulped everything down at last, I cried out, 'Marika!' You raised me up from my knees then and kissed me. Tears mingled with our kisses. We didn't know from which of us they came.

"You know, Hungarian, I felt in my bones then that we belonged to each other for the rest of our lives. I can't remember now what we said to each other, except that the words were loving and sprang from hearts full of happiness——"

"But I can still remember what you said, Unholy George," the Hungarian interrupted. " 'Marika,' you said, 'don't be angry with me for being away so long!' And I answered that I would love you so much that the three bad years would soon be forgotten . . ."

There was a pause. After a while I found the Hungarian standing in front of me. She took my head between her loyal little hands.

"Dear Unholy George, carry me upstairs!"

I lifted her up in my arms, taking no notice whatever of my weak ankle. We climbed the staircase to the bliss of the night.

10

Lois came over next morning quite early, when he knew I should be in the stable with the Majestic One. He had brought the sign boards with him, hidden under his jacket. He had the mottoes for the front door and the stable door, the one for the living room, and also that for the bedroom upstairs. I really felt almost remorseful about my secret plan when I read the latter. But Lois had painted it so splendidly that it would be a real ornament to the wall and we decided to put it up at once. The meaning of the motto was quite fiendishly immoral. It was expressed in these terms:

"Who seeks women and horses that none can e'er vie with
Neither steed has in stable nor angel to lie with!"

The beauty of Lois's colored lettering did away with the element of sacrilege in the motto.

"Come on, then, let's hang it up!" said Lois.

"Yes, but the two mottoes for the rooms will have to be smuggled in somehow. If the Hungarian finds out about them first, we're done!"

"You're right there," Lois said. "Women always have to be faced with the accomplished fact!"

We hid those two not exactly house-trained mottoes in the oat bin and started giving the others the freedom of the premises. I held the ladder and Lois nailed them up on high. The Majestic One got the verses about the earthly paradise and we stuck the other over the front door. They showed up very well. They were most decorative ornaments and at the same time highly significant.

All undertakings need luck to succeed, particularly when you want to catch someone napping with them. The Hungarian emerged from the kitchen to say that we couldn't go on any longer with the whisk in that state. The whisk was a product of my own craftsmanship. I had made it out of a superannuated Christmas tree, turning it upside down and pruning the branches to form the whisk, while the trunk served as the handle. Well, now it wouldn't work any more and the Hungarian wanted to go to Hansl's, the village general store, and buy a proper whisk. I encouraged her to do so, simply to get her out of the house in quick time. She hadn't reached the gate of the front garden before we started carting those crazy mottoes into the room. By the time she returned we had assumed perfectly innocent expressions again. She quite liked the notices over the front door and the stable. But she hadn't yet seen, thank heaven, the ones we had put up inside the house.

"What about the one for Farmer Schwaiger?" I asked Lois.

"It's up already, I fixed it last night."

I gave him a good scolding, for I'd very much wanted to be in on that. But he told me that, with my bad ankle, I might not perhaps have been able to make such a quick getaway if Schwaiger had happened to spot anything.

There was a bit of a fuss, all the same, over our nice new mottoes. First of all the priest arrived and told us that the one over the front door was quite unsuitable for a Catholic neighborhood. He said it was by Dr. Martin Luther, who had ruined the trade in indulgences run by the Pope of his day.

"If Luther invented sayings like that, he's the boy for me!" I retorted. "It doesn't worry me what his beliefs may have been. Don't you start any religious wars with me, Father!"

He said it was just like me to talk like that, for I had never been anything but a dummy in church and entertained pagan beliefs which he was very sorry indeed to see. As he wouldn't stop preaching to me, I finally had to tell him that all the mottoes came from his own book. I threatened to cut off supplies of that wine which had done him so much good as to enable him to sleep through an occurrence like a horse's wedding in the open street, which must otherwise have been so offensive to him.

That silenced him. So as to give him yet another shock right away, we confronted him with the motto in the living room, the one about the three kicking things in this world.

Of course he started off again at once with his wrangling about its being improper. He made such a row that the Hungarian came in to see what the fuss was all about.

As she didn't want to begin quarreling with me, in a fashion which could not be matrimonial, in front of the priest, she said she liked the motto and added that so far as it was concerned with wine she thought it extremely accurate. She smiled charmingly at the priest as she spoke, with the result that he declared he would withdraw his objection if the Countess considered the motto unexceptionable.

Peace had only just been restored when Farmer Schwaiger, who had already been across to see Lois, appeared at the window, shouting out that he would have his blood.

The priest at once forbade him, in the first place, to use such un-Christian language. Then he demanded a statement of the facts. Schwaiger explained that someone had nailed a vulgar inscription over his front door, of so obscene a character that it was the priest's duty to come and read it himself. Personally, he had not noticed it at all. But that old gossip of a postmaster had been the first to see it, and now the whole village knew about it. They kept sending one another to go and read the notice.

Lois said it was Schwaiger's business to prove his accusation.

But the latter only stuck to it that Lois had done the job and said he also strongly suspected myself.

The priest decided to investigate the facts on the spot. So off we went, all five of us, the Hungarian coming, too, which made me extremely uneasy.

A dense crowd had gathered in front of Schwaiger's house. His wife was screaming abuse at them from an upstairs window, calling them a shameless set of ragamuffins and ordering them to clear out.

The priest and the Hungarian flushed when they read that highly flavored stuff about frontages and hindquarters. Lois laughed himself sick. I said I shouldn't like to have anything of that sort on my house. For the Hungarian's sake I, too, had to give utterance to a certain amount of moral indignation.

Lois said that it was he, in fact, who had painted the sign board. But he added that he hadn't put it there. Someone had ordered the thing from him, without saying what it was for.

Schwaiger wanted to know the impudent rascal's name. But Lois replied that he was in honor bound not to reveal the identity of his patron.

Aha, said Schwaiger. In that case he knew well enough who was at the bottom of it. He was sworn enemies with only three people. To make sure of punishing the guilty party he intended to tan the hides of all three of them till he broke every bone in their bodies.

It was the priest, once more, who opposed this notion. His view was that the law alone could intervene in this case. But Schwaiger wouldn't have anything to do with the law, ever since his denial on oath of paternity in the affiliation suit brought by Josepha, who lived in the next village. That affair had nearly got him into serious trouble and cost him a mint of money before he could find someone else to assume responsibility and pay up. The whole truth of the matter was never discovered, for Schwaiger got his hackles up the moment anyone even happened to mention maintenance allowances.

The priest decided, accordingly, that in any case the first thing was to take the notice down. Lois therefore himself removed the scandalous sign which his own mischievous hands had previously set in position.

He's a cunning devil! He handled the pliers so clumsily that he split the board. When he came down from the ladder he said a thing like that ought to be burned. Before anyone could object he had thrown it into Schwaiger's kitchen range, thus disposing for good of the principal exhibit in the case.

"Let's beat it," said I to the Hungarian. We began to walk away. Lois and the priest, finding nothing better to do, joined us. The priest said he considered Lois and myself to have been the originators of this unpleasant affair. But the Hungarian was able to bear witness that I had never left the house but, on the contrary, had slept, as usual, beside her.

The reference to sleeping together which the Hungarian uttered in such a matter-of-fact manner made the priest wince. For we had only been united in matrimony under the eyes of the Almighty, not those of the priest. Consequently, he now got his teeth into Lois, who in his turn produced Mirl as chief witness for the defense. As those two were in the same parlous situation as ourselves, the priest did not enlarge, for the time being, on that aspect of the matter. He said, however, that if the case ever came into court, the truth would have to come out.

"Well, you can see for yourself that the truth wouldn't do Schwaiger much good," said Lois. "Personally, I don't believe he'll ever risk a show-down. He'd rather rough-house it and get a good leathering himself and serve him right!"

The priest talked about one black sheep contaminating the whole flock. It was all he could think of for the moment. Actually, he had been to blame for the whole business. What did he want to lend us that wicked horse book for? What did he mean by keeping such forbidden works in his house? Of course, the one the score should really be chalked up to was Mohammed, with his donkeys and camels. If he had ridden a horse, like a decent fellow, this complicated affair of the sign board could never have arisen, because then the priest, with his eternal craze for being right, would not have brought us the book.

"At bottom, it was all the fault of that fool of a Mussulman!" I exclaimed aloud. The priest only gave me a vindictive look and then disappeared, with a "God be with you!" into his house.

The Hungarian had, of course, already guessed the truth. I had shared in concocting the original idea and Lois had done everything else.

And that motto in the living room, she added, was not just exactly to her taste either.

"Take it down then," I said.

"No, we'll keep it there," she retorted, "as an eternal reminder to both of you of your deed of shame!"

"So you do like it really," Lois remarked.

The Hungarian told him to clear off back to his Mirl. So Lois departed, glad to get off so cheaply, and leaving me to face my inevitable fear that the Hungarian, now she had me to herself, would start one of her lectures.

But once again she took a wholly unexpected course and said nothing more about the affair. Apparently she had given up the attempt to convert me to an irreproachable mode of life. All the same I wished I could manage to take that motto off the wall in the bedroom upstairs and thus be spared the final settlement of accounts, which would involve reinvestigation of all outstanding items.

"Lois is no sort of a companion for you," she observed, in an incidental sort of way.

"You must be patient with Unholy George, Hungarian," I answered.

"Now that we've been nine years together I've got pretty used to that!" was her reply.

"If it weren't for you, I'm quite certain I should end up in jail," I said remorsefully.

"So long as you realize it . . ."

"You're content, eh?"

"Living with you certainly teaches one not to expect too much!" she retorted, smiling.

"You see? I've got a good influence on you, too, Hungarian, in that respect!"

"Give me a kiss. That'll stop you talking, at any rate!" she said, as we arrived at the front door.

"Well, if I must," I answered, "I will!"

When I bent to kiss her, after we had entered the house, she bit my nose. The Hungarian can play some nasty tricks when she likes!

11

"*W*ell," I began, that evening, resuming the story, "you've already said yourself what happened next, Hungarian. You were due to leave for Budapest that day and had only been waiting for me so that I should not find the house empty when I arrived. A few hours later we were sitting in the National Hotel, listening to the gypsy orchestra. After we had gone upstairs, I felt like nothing on earth. I shouldn't have come to your room at all in such a state——"

"Oh, stop talking about that, Unholy George, it's forgotten long ago! You really mustn't be perpetually dwelling on these unfortunate episodes!" the Hungarian interrupted.

"Well, you've already mentioned our night on the Puszta, too," I went on. "And that was really the first of the right sort that we had together. You were quite different then, Hungarian, when——"

"Unholy George!" she cried, getting in my way again. "Talk about the Majestic One now! How we got on at that time we both know, and——"

"But don't you think it was a wonderful experience, Hungarian?"

"Well, of course it was!" she rejoined, laughing. "But you don't need to give an account of historic events at which we were both present. There's no point in it!"

"Aha," I commented. "So this evening the story won't be a very long one, eh?"

The Hungarian looked at me with an angry smile. Her trick of smiling charmingly when she is angry is inimitable. I don't think she could ever manage it, either, before we met. I believe she learned it by living with me.

"The Majestic One joined the herd of horses on the Puszta. He so enjoyed the wide open spaces that he gave the easygoing Janos endless trouble. The Majestic One would simply gallop away. And Janos' horse couldn't catch him up. Again and again a wild pursuit followed. As soon as Janos and his horse were both utterly exhausted, the Majestic One would make a wide circle and return to the herd, where he put on the most innocent airs. But Janos bore him no malice. He said that he personally considered the Majestic One the finest horse in the world.

"I stayed with you for a whole year, Hungarian. As we

were able to share the work on the estate, we often had an entire day free to spend together. I often thought, you know, how short a time it was that we had been acquainted. And yet it was as though we had been made for each other——"

"No other woman would have put up with you for so long, let me tell you," observed the Hungarian, who seemed determined to prevent me getting on with the story that evening.

"What a thing to say!" I exclaimed. "Why, the first few days and weeks had scarcely passed before you felt as though we had always been together. I often used to think, myself, that we must have met in some previous existence."

"I suppose we used to be a couple of cab horses in Vienna, running in double harness?" the Hungarian enquired. "Do you know that today you're talking the most utter rubbish, Unholy George?"

"Maybe, but I'm just coming to the time now when I had to leave, Hungarian. Give me a chance!"

"No, you let me tell," she said. "I'm just in the mood now. One day a letter came from Leopold in Vienna, with another inside it, an official one, saying that you had come into money. Your Uncle Xaver, to whom this house and ground used to belong, had died, after being unable to find a better man than yourself to leave all his property to. So of course you had to go and see about it. Family feeling required your presence, and the cash, too, would come in useful. So one day Janos drove you to the station at Kecskemét and I stood at the gate and waved until I lost sight of you. The place immediately began to seem very empty, Unholy George, I must confess. It was a bit of luck that I still had the Majestic One. You know, it often quite frightened me to think that perhaps you might not come back, not because you didn't want to, but because something unforeseen might happen. Well, two weeks went by and you really didn't come back. You only sent a letter to say that you would still be some time, as you would be bringing a young lady with you. I thought you must have also inherited a child born to Uncle Xaver in his old age, and thus nearly missing the boat altogether. I supposed that, not knowing what to do with her, you were going to bring her along, thinking that Marika would take her on all right, but all the same——"

"Here, let me go on again now," I exclaimed and continued rapidly, so that she couldn't interrupt me. "You forgot to say that you had made me a present of the Majestic One. I was delighted. But it tortured me to think that I couldn't give you anything better in return than myself and that you would thus be to a certain extent out of pocket on my account. I'd been working quite hard, you must admit that. But all the same, I did feel I was a miserable sort of creature, a kind of princess' favorite——"

"A pauper Countess', you mean," remarked the Hungarian.

"Well, when I found myself in possession of Uncle Xaver's legacy, the money was there all right, but the house was in a ghastly state of rack and ruin. Then all of a sudden I had a brilliant idea. I would repair the house and garden and as soon as it was all ready I would bring the Hungarian over to see the kind of home I had. It was then that I made friends with Lois and the two of us set to work like fiends. In two weeks we had everything ready and it didn't cost so very much after all, for Lois is an inventive sort of chap, very knowledgeable about repairs and a thousand other craftsmen's jobs. Then I wondered what I was to do with the rest of the money. I've never been thrilled at the idea of having money in the cupboard or at the bank, I've always splurged it immediately. On this occasion, I decided, I was going to spend it on the Hungarian. I thought of all sorts of things and racked my brains. But as I couldn't imagine you with a pearl necklace, I came to the conclusion that it would have to be something quite out of the ordinary. I went to Vienna and confided in Leopold. He solved the problem straight away.

" 'What can anyone give a horse-crazy female but a horse?' he demanded.

" 'Good God! Deflorata!' I shouted.

"Next day we called at the Ministry. Eventually we extracted permission for me to buy Deflorata. So you see, Hungarian, it really was on account of the young lady that I had to take another week!"

"You sent a telegram later to say you wanted to be fetched from the station," the Hungarian said. "When I arrived I couldn't get down from the carriage because the Majestic One, whom I had harnessed in honor of the occasion, refused to come to terms with his trappings. Meanwhile the train had gone on, the last of the passengers had alighted, and you were not among them. I was just going to drive off in a rage when you turned up, leading Deflorata and waving your hat, that dark one, incidentally, which I never could stand. The Majestic One must immediately have recognized Deflorata and she him. They neighed and rubbed noses together. We two didn't get a chance to exchange a kiss of welcome until Deflorata had been put in the shafts next to the Majestic One and you had climbed on to the driving seat.

" 'I'm making you a present of her, Hungarian!' you said, beaming all over your face.

" 'Well, that certainly is nice of you,' I answered. 'Did you spend the entire legacy on one horse?'

" 'You can turn me upside-down if you like and keep everything that falls out of my pockets!' you replied. I knew then that you had used up all your money to give me pleasure, Unholy George. You went on to tell me that you had become a householder and that I should have to come and see your place.

"On the drive home we drew up, there and then, the whole plan for our future existence. We were going to start a breeding establishment for Lipizzaners. I would see about getting another mare for us, from Esterhazy, or else try our luck at the Bábolna auction sale, where we might be able to pick up a good horse. The Majestic One and Deflorata, at four years old, were still only children and there could be no question of their founding a family as yet. You then began about us, Unholy George. Wouldn't it be a good thing if we, too, founded a family? I was pleased to hear you suggest such a thing, but I couldn't believe that I should feel any happier if I were your wife, duly signed, sealed, and delivered. Well, Unholy George, I told you, if I ever get to the stage of needing a name for a child, you can give him yours and give it to me, too, eh? But as a matter of fact it didn't turn out that way. Never mind, don't take it too badly, Unholy George, we've still got our four-legged children anyhow, thank heaven!"

She stopped speaking and I lifted her chin to make her look at me.

"Happiness must always be paid for, Marika, my Hungarian," I said. "Nothing is ever gratis. We are happy in each other and in our horses. And our happiness is so great that the Lord probably thinks we should get swelled heads if He sent us any more happiness in the shape of children."

The Hungarian took my hand and laid her lips upon it.

"You're an Unholy George," said she. "And yet you can talk like a saint when you like. That's not too bad, I think. Meanwhile, go ahead with the story!"

"Our two Lipizzaners joined the herd. Boy-horse and girl-horse became inseparable. They always grazed close to each other. Whenever one of the browns or blacks tried to interfere with them, they resisted in common. Deflorata lashed out with her hind legs and the Majestic One charged the enemy with his forefeet in the air.

"But at last that glorious life on the Puszta had to come to an end. The nobler the horse, the stricter the training he has to undergo. One day Janos was ordered to bring the Majestic One to the estate. There we tried to saddle him.

"Janos held him while you talked to him in a soothing tone, telling him there was nothing to worry about, and I laid the saddle, with extreme caution, across his back, behind the withers. The Majestic One did not feel quite at his ease, but as he had hitherto never experienced anything disagreeable at human hands, he only had that peculiar sensation we ourselves are aware of when we have to take our seat in a dentist's chair.

"I then very gently tightened the girths, only just enough to keep the saddle in position. He knew about the bridle because it was used with the halter. The only unfamiliar thing was that thick mouthpiece, the bit. But he readily opened his mouth and allowed the cold iron to be thrust into it. Before he knew what had happened he was saddled and bridled, I had him on the lunging rein and was making him run round me in a circle. You manipulated the long whip, to keep his hoofbeats steady, and even on that first day he didn't do so badly. But sometimes he gave way to high spirits, suddenly leaping in the air, trying to start a tug-of-war with me on the lunging rein or bucking against the saddle in most unmajestic fashion. 'Hey, Majestic One!' you would call out then, whereupon he seemed rather ashamed of himself and resumed his modest pace, so I could tell him later on that he had put up a good show. We didn't have a great deal of bother with him. You might almost say he was ridden as soon as he became a stallion. He always held his muzzle in the correct position, at a slight angle to the perpendicular, and we didn't need any auxiliary reins. All we did was to have a curb sent out from Budapest, to guard against any possible awkwardness of mine in pulling too hard at his mouth when he was on the lunging rein.

"One day you said I ought to start riding him. He had grown strong enough to carry me and he was familiar with everything a riding horse should know.

"Well, so we risked it. You held him and Janos helped me to mount. I let myself down into the saddle very gently and tentatively, like a man in the dark cautiously sitting down on what he believes to be a chair, though a shaky one.

"Then we were ready for anything. But the Majestic One

stood perfectly still. I slapped his neck and said, 'You see, we stuck it out! Good lad, Majestic One!'

"He snorted. To keep him in a good temper, you had the idea of giving him a lump of sugar, the first he had ever tasted. He found it had a very queer flavor. But with angelic patience you put it back again into his mouth every time he dropped it. The lump soon dissolved and I suddenly noticed that the Majestic One was taking a deep breath. I took up the reins and at the same moment he spat all the juice of the sugar into our worthy Janos' face, plastering both eyes and his mustache with it.

"Then the Majestic One dashed off with me in a wild series of leaps, till I had to stand in the stirrups to prevent myself being thrown across him in spread-eagle fashion. You were helping Janos to haul on the lunging rein and it was a bit of luck, in the end, that the hook flew out of the curb ring. The two of us were out of the gate in a flash and away, hell for leather, into the Puszta. He wasn't bucking now, but simply galloping for all he was worth. He didn't take the slightest notice of either rein or thigh signals. There could be no two opinions about it. The Majestic One had lost his head. He was bolting.

"I was in no hurry, however. So far as I was concerned he could gallop to the end of the world. He was bound to tire after a while. I meant to ride him home then, and at the same pace as he had run for it. After that he would lose his taste for bolting.

"Well, he did come to his senses shortly afterward, reflecting that it had been silly to use up valuable energy like that. It began to run short, too, that valuable energy. His leaps covered less ground. Only his hind legs were galloping now, while his forelegs merely trotted. At last he came to a halt, shaking his head.

" 'You are a young fool, Majestic One,' I told him, as I slapped his neck. He tried to turn his head to look at me. He'd quite forgotten all about me when he took leave of his senses. It was only the weight and that lump of sugar to which he had been unaccustomed.

"But I didn't give him much time to get his second wind. Up to now he'd been running to please himself. It was my turn now and I wanted to ride home. He had to start by trotting in the style he had learned on the lunging rein. Then, to make it easier for him, I let him gallop. But soon, in his desire to come to a standstill, his paces shortened. Then the pressure of my thighs would impel him on again. No doubt he came to realize in time that the thigh movements were made to give him support, not to annoy him. His fatigue caused him to try and use the bit as a fifth leg to help him along. But as I alternately relaxed and tightened my hold of it by the reins, he soon learned of his own accord to respond to the rein movement and began to champ the bit. In order to let him know that he was doing the right thing, I dismounted and walked with him, for the last half-hour, to the house. You had watched us from the gate, Hungarian, when we left, and now that we were returning safe and sound you were laughing, for a weight had fallen from your heart. You gave him another lump of sugar, because you wanted to find out whether he had possibly grown a bit sulky and weary of everything. But the Majestic One accepted the sugar readily and chewed it. He probably thought that sugar and riding went together and he was obviously going to develop a taste for sugar, as a young man does for smoking. Unfortunately he soon got so accustomed to it that nowadays he begs for it, in most unmajestic fashion, from everyone he meets.

"He certainly began to get bored with riding during the next few days, for we made no more excursions into the Puszta but simply went round and round the sandy arena in the courtyard. To prevent his taking it into his head to bolt again, or relieve himself of his esteemed burden, Janos always held the lunging rein. In time the Majestic One became the quietest horse to ride that anyone could wish. It is true that he developed a certain sensitivity and was easily put out. I myself had to learn how best to treat him. One cut I gave him with the switch to make him pay the necessary attention impressed him deeply. He didn't try to retaliate and he didn't buck. He merely, so to speak, rebuked me with his disdain. He didn't, of course, change his behavior toward you, Hungarian. He nuzzled your cheek, as usual, with his velvety muzzle. But as for me, he looked over my head as if I had been his groom. It didn't last long, though. When we rode out into the Puszta and spent the night with the cattlemen, he slept beside me and woke me in the morning with the familiar caress.

"Deflorata used to be driven in the gig at this time. She had a very graceful knee action. She had already been making up to the Majestic One. But he, the innocent simpleton, still didn't know he was a stallion.

"One day Ferencz, formerly of the Spanish Riding School in Vienna, paid us a visit from Budapest. After riding the Majestic One he told us we really ought to have him trained at the School.

"He said that if Leopold could be persuaded to take the

Majestic One at the Riding School I shouldn't recognize my own horse when he returned. Ferencz added that I was making the work too easy for him and that he would never get on, at any rate never become a champion, while he was with me. 'All right,' I answered. 'Let's have him trained, then!' The Majestic One made me a distinctly poor return for this decision. Ferencz suggested that I should mount him while Janos cracked the whip to speed up the Majestic One's circulation. I should then see, said Ferencz, what sort of a horse I had between my knees, for mere excitement would cause him, of his own accord, to perform the Spanish Walk.

"Unfortunately the worthy Janos had miscalculated the length of the whiplash. In cracking it he inadvertently stung the Majestic One's hindquarters. The horse reared and bucked, while I laboriously collected a handful of his mane to hold, so as not to saw his mouth. At the same time I kicked off my stirrups. Ferencz rushed up to seize the reins, but the Majestic One dug in his forelegs, bringing me down upon his neck, and at the same instant leaping at Ferencz. I was thrown backward and slid out of the saddle, striking the ground first with the back of my hand and then with my skull, whereupon it seemed as though someone had turned out the light in my brain.

"Later on I found myself lying, with my head and chest soaking wet, on a horse blanket under the ancient tree in the courtyard. The first thing I saw was your eyes, Hungarian. And, seeing them, it's easy for anyone to smile, even if every bone in his body is aching. It was you who had fetched the blanket and made me comfortable on it, while Ferencz had poured two buckets of water over my head and chest to bring me back to my senses. It was positively touching to see what a fuss you two were making about me."

"You may laugh now," interposed the Hungarian, "but I was in quite a panic about you at the time. From the way you fell I was afraid you could never get over it. 'Dear God,' I thought, 'you have only just given him to me and now you take him away again! Please keep him for me!'"

At this point she felt ashamed of having let me see so deep into her heart. She added: "Do go on with the story now, will you?"

"Well, I still had that tuft of the Majestic One's mane in my hand. After a time I was hauled to my feet. 'Do you know,' I said, 'I believe my whole crupper's twisted!'

"You wanted to put me straight to bed. But first I had to go to the Majestic One and let him know that we were still on friendly terms. I think he himself was sorry to see me come limping over. He pushed his muzzle against my cheek and rubbed his head on my sleeve. Then Ferencz said he would have to catch the train back to Budapest, and Janos, who had sworn that he would have hanged himself if the lieutenant had gone to hell, was obliged to harness the carriage horses at once.

"Later on we made an inspection of my crupper. There was a bruise right across it as big as a dinner plate. When you started to massage it, we found it was movable. That actually made you laugh, Hungarian. You simply, heartlessly, laughed!"

"That was only to cheer you up, you know. You gave such a fearful groan when I touched it!"

"There were loud rejoicings on your part that the swelling could be moved so easily. The same day you wrote to Leopold to ask whether we could send him the Majestic One for training. We didn't get an answer for a long time. But eventually he wrote that we could bring him. As he was a Lipizzaner, he could, as a special favor, attend the Spanish Riding School. And Leopold added that he hoped to see us soon, as he would like to visit the vineyards with us again. But it wasn't such a simple matter for us to get away. First Janos had to receive precise instructions as to his duties in the capacity of estate steward. You remarked that it would be easier for him if he had a woman's help. Janos replied that he would see what could be done in that respect. A girl he had known for a long time had quite recently given him the glad eye in Kecskemét. If they could hit it off together he would be willing to marry her. But first he would have to see what she was like at work and also on other occasions. He brought her out the very next day. You had a chat with her and thought she might get on very well with Janos.

"Accordingly, we set off on our journey with our minds at rest. As Istvan, the groom, was leading out the Majestic One, he passed the loose-box. Deflorata looked out over the door and neighed after the Majestic One in a low tone. But he never answered——"

"You male types are all like that," said the Hungarian. "Once you can get away you forget everything you leave behind!"

"That would be another marvelous sentence to end up with, Hungarian," I said, yawning.

"All right, if you're sleepy, come on then, let's go!" she answered.

In the bedroom upstairs the ceiling light didn't go on. By way of precaution I had unscrewed the globe.

It looked to me as if we should have to go to bed in the dark, as—by an extraordinary coincidence!—the lamps on the bedside tables didn't go on either!

But the Hungarian insisted on having some light. She said my place had all the worst features of a bachelor establishment. Before I could stop her she had climbed on to the bed and screwed in the globe. Of course she instantly spotted the signboard with that profane motto on it.

She shook her head, exclaiming:

"I wonder you didn't have the pillows embroidered with mottoes while you were about it! You're a terrific pair, you two, with your mottoes! Each one's wickeder than the last. Did you ever hear of such a thing? An angel to lie with, indeed!"

"You could have one in a four-poster, you know, with a canopy, because there's the canopy of heaven, where the angels——"

"I'll give you angels, you ruffian! You don't get over me with your indecent mottoes!"

She chucked all the pillows at my head and I chucked them back at her. Soon all the feathers began to come out and the Hungarian at once started worrying about the waste of valuable down.

She snatched the split head pillow away from me and told me I could lay my weary napper to rest somewhere else.

Later on, just as we were going to sleep, I found the mattress really a bit too hard for my head. I shifted over to the Hungarian's side.

"Let's have a bit of your pillow, my angel!"

She must have been very tired, for she made room for me, murmuring, "Fancy calling me an angel! When I've got so many faults!"

12

$\mathcal{I}$n the summer Lois and I, they say, are the most photographed men in the whole district. The pasture in which we do our mowing is close to the forest path, which is a favorite walk for summer visitors.

Sometimes, when we're mowing, either Lois or I will say, "Look, there's another one coming!"

We immediately stop working. Lois starts whetting the blade of his scythe on the stone. I scrutinize the sky for possible changes in the weather, adopting a highly picturesque attitude, with my hand shading my eyes. One of us keeps squinting at the road and as soon as the male or female tripper focuses the camera we stand as still as statues.

We've already once reached the pages of the local rag in this fashion, the caption stating that we were the scions of a mighty race and of course adding the usual drivel about features hewn as though from a block of wood.

When we drive the Majestic One out in a hired vehicle to cut kale, we always have a bet about how many photographs will be taken of us that day. We usually overestimate the number though.

While the scythes hiss through the grass we whistle a bit or discuss some project we intend to carry out together.

"I say, I'm getting on quite well with Saint George," said Lois one day.

"Well, you've taken enough photographs, anyhow," I retorted. "You were snapping away like a summer visitor! Shown anything to the priest yet?"

"No, but he keeps prowling round my place like a fox after geese. I shan't show him anything till it's all ready."

"I hope you'll get it done before I leave with the Hungarian and the stallion."

"I think I shall," returned Lois. "Hallo, there comes somebody!"

I immediately stood up to look at the weather and Lois began whetting his scythe. Then he stared up at the sky in his turn and I whetted, as on this occasion my blade really needed it.

"All over," Lois said suddenly. "Photo's taken."

So we went back to our work.

"I shall be interested to hear what they say about my

Saint George, with that female on his saddle bow," Lois observed.

"I'm afraid that, with you on the job, the whole group will turn out distinctly voluptuous," I told him.

"Certainly not," Lois reassured me. "There's such an air of sanctity about your three wooden heads that merely to look at them would make anyone feel devout. I consider, in fact, that I've won the right to eternal bliss with the thing . . . ah, curse and damn it all. . . ."

Lois went on swearing a lot more after this reference to eternal bliss. What he said was quite unprintable. But he did have a reason for doing so, as everyone must freely admit. He had hacked the blade of his scythe against a cunning beast of a stone that was lying in the grass. The blade now looked like an old saw.

"Don't let it get you down," I said. "I was just going to pack up, anyhow."

"You might have told me that before. Then I should never have hit the blasted thing."

"Oh, put a sock in it!" I retorted. I called the Majestic One, to make him come over with the cart, for loading up. We hadn't been cutting grass for him but for Mirl's three goats, which we couldn't let into the pasture, as they were liable to bolt, taking their tethers and pegs with them.

The Majestic One had eaten such a bellyful of grass that his girth was near to bursting. After we had loaded up and were driving home we met another of those holiday-making females.

The Majestic One was trudging along, with his head and even his ears hanging down. We two were sitting on the load of grass, exactly as townspeople are in the habit of imagining yokels on their way home. I was holding the driving rein in my dirty paws, adopting such a weary attitude that it was practically trailing over the footrest. Lois had the scythes under his arm and was puffing thick clouds of smoke from a pipe of prodigious size.

Now and again we cast wary glances at the state of the weather.

"Hey, Lois," I muttered. "Summat comin' up!"

We pulled up close to that holiday-making female.

"What say, stoopid?" Lois demanded.

"Summat comin', ye fool," I repeated.

"Ain't nuthin', I say!"

"An' I say there be! You tell me again there ain't nuthin', I'll clout ye one!"

The summer visitor waited to see whether we would come to blows.

"Wouldn't nuthin' come from thataway nohow!" scoffed Lois.

"Year eighty it come from there, I tell ye!" I retorted, and went on to say that Farmer Seppl's "little hut" had been struck head-on by lightning in that year.

Thereupon Lois coarsely added that Farmer Seppl himself had been squatting in that "little hut" at the time, on a place where one expects to be left in peace.

He then turned to the attentively listening tripper, who came from up north by the look of her. He fixed her with a glittering eye.

"Ought to 'a' seen that, ye ought! Sepp run through the village holdin' up his britches an' a yellin' the lightnin' it catched his backside, see!"

The northerner obviously hadn't understood him, for she

laughed, a thing no lady would have done if she had known what he was talking about.

Then she asked what the weather was going to be. Would it be nice? If so, she'd stay another week.

"Wot, this comin' week?" I said. "Orful! Fair orful!"

"Get on, ye crazy bastard!" grunted Lois at my elbow. As I didn't want the summer visitor to think he meant her, I told the Majestic One to go ahead.

Couldn't we give her a lift into the village? she asked. Her feet were hurting so!

"Sure," I said.

"You got corns and bunions all right! Saw that, I did, right away," said Lois. Then he asked her where she was staying.

She answered, at Mr. Schwaiger's.

"Ah, he'll see ye right," Lois said. I gave him such an obvious nudge in the ribs that the northerner couldn't help seeing it.

What did we mean, she wanted to know.

"He's not as bad as they tell," Lois explained. "Though I reckon no woman safe when he's about!"

"Mind ye lock your door, missis," I added, to give her a real good dressing of gooseflesh.

"I ain't said nuthin', though. Nuthin' at all I ain't," Lois warned her.

"Not me neither," I said.

After that we were quiet for a bit. Then, all of a sudden, Lois began to speak quite up-to-date High German. Did I think, he asked, that he ought to use a tempera medium for the picture he had been commissioned by the government to paint? And how did I like the perspective and composition so far?

I replied that Michelangelo had always brought his perspective into proper relation with his composition and that if Lois couldn't do such a thing he could only be regarded as an ignorant amateur.

The northerner, in her amazement, forgot to keep her mouth shut.

"Oh! You gentlemen are artists, native to this district?" she asked.

"What's that she says?" Lois demanded in dialect, addressing me. "That we're natives, Comanches, Igorots? And artists? Ay, we're artists all right, artists in hunger, when we can't get anything to eat! And you tell her something else, too. There's going to be blue murder when our wives see us cartin' strange women about!"

It wasn't necessary for me to translate that into High German for the northerner.

She at once insisted upon our stopping and letting her get down. We were only too delighted to do so. All the same, as soon as she had alighted she called after us that we were a couple of impudent louts.

"There you are," said Lois. "Ingratitude was ever the way of this world."

When we told Mirl and the Hungarian, who happened to be with her at the time, the whole truth about our adventure, the Hungarian said that the lady from the north had been perfectly right.

The priest had been asking every day what the position was about his getting his book back. I started by telling him, quite untruly, that our respected friend the Hungarian

Countess was still reading it, to which he answered that he wished he could sink through the floor. He didn't do so, however. He returned the following day and made a scene with me. He had found out that the book was at Lois' place. Mirl had told him so.

"Well, you go and get it from Lois, Father," I suggested.

"No! I lent it to you and it's your business to give it back to me," he insisted.

"All right then, go and lodge a complaint against me at the Prince Archbishop's office in Salzburg, if you like. But you'd better get it from Lois!"

He wouldn't hear of applying to Salzburg. The book wasn't that kind of a book at all. He was in an awful stew over those five mottoes, because, although they weren't quite decent, they were nevertheless unquestionably traditional.

So it would have gone on probably for quite a time if the Hungarian, who must have got wind of the situation, had not intervened. One day she marched over to Lois' place, snatched the book from him, and gave it to the priest.

In doing so she told him that she hoped he would never again lend books of that sort to such childishly irresponsible people. The priest left her presence profoundly abashed, feeling that nothing would ever be the same again now that even the Hungarian was being sarcastic with him.

She still seemed to be in rather a touchy mood that evening. Didn't I think it was about time I went on with the story, or did I intend to spin it out till the Day of Judgment? I ought really now to try and get a good solid bit of it done instead of for ever creating scandals in the village.

So I started off straight away with the narrative, as if I were being paid to do it.

"Well, then, when we arrived in Vienna with the Majestic One——"

"Don't skip like that!" she interrupted. "How did we get there?"

"Oh yes, of course! We traveled with the Majestic One in his truck."

"All right. Go on, then."

"Right. But if the flow of my narrative's constantly being held up, naturally I can't get on with it," I retorted. As she didn't answer, I went on:

"Leopold then took the Majestic One in hand. On the very first day he declared that our stallion would have to be turned into a horse before anything could be done with him. He didn't leave him a single redeeming feature and laid all the blame on me. He did say, however, when he saw me looking so miserable: 'Don't put on that idiotic expression! Lovers always make bad tutors. You can't expect to be the only exception!'

"In any case he started again with the Majestic One from scratch. He put him on the lunging rein until he had learned to trot in really elegant fashion. Leopold told us both that we only made the Majestic One nervous by coming every day to watch. He added that we got on his own nerves, too. If we came back in six months, he said, we should be doing a very great service both to him and to the Majestic One.

"I then suggested to you that we might as well pay a visit to my own property. You smiled more charmingly, when you heard me use that expression, than you have all today, Hungarian. . . ."

She trod on my toes, smiled charmingly, and signed to me, with a twinkle, to proceed.

"We came by the slow train. Lois met us at the station in an ancient, springless cart he had borrowed from the postmaster. The horse looked as if it were suffering from consumption.

"Lois said he had bought up the beast from a grocer in Salzburg, simply out of pity, to give the poor old crock a home.

"I examined the animal's mouth. You also inspected it and said you had never seen such a Methuselah of a horse. We preferred not to get into the cart and told Lois that he would also have to walk, leaving our two suitcases as the only passengers. Accordingly, we drove into the village on foot. Whenever there was a slight uphill gradient, you took over the reins and Lois and I had to push behind.

" 'Lois, the poor brute hasn't got a single tooth left in his head!'

" 'I know,' Lois answered. 'Mirl always feeds him on porridge.'

" 'You're a good man,' you told Lois, Hungarian."

"I recant that opinion here and now!" she exclaimed. "And you're just such another good-for-nothing!"

I don't like to hear people talking of me in that way. So I went on at once.

"Naturally, the whole village knew we were coming, as I had telegraphed to Lois, and so the postmaster knew all about it.

"When we arrived, they were all on their doorsteps. The

priest himself was there to welcome us, for he, too, felt curious about the foreigner I was bringing with me.

"Then I carried you over the threshold, exactly as if we had been going to be married. That was what the priest thought, evidently, for he called later and asked whether you had yet arranged for accommodation. He said he could put you up in his spare room. At this we both laughed and you said you were just going to stay with Unholy George. The priest asked whom you meant. You pointed to me and he made a face as if he had bitten a peppercorn. He had to gulp it down, just the same!

"By the following day you had already put the house in order. Not a single stick of furniture was left in its original position. By the time everything had been changed round at least twice, you said that things would now for the first time be arranged in a reasonably convenient way.

"Immediately afterward you started to plant the rock garden. Your fingernails became permanently black. Lois and I had to go scrambling up into the mountains to get you a genuine Alpine gentian and an edelweiss. The latter, however, we didn't gather ourselves, but bought in Salzburg, Lois having convinced me that it would be positively sinful to break one's neck just for the sake of a rockery."

"The shameless scamp!" said the Hungarian. "Well, go on. I wonder what's going to come out next!"

"Nothing, Hungarian. That was only a slip of the tongue on my part. Well, it took you less than three days to feel quite at home in the village, as though you had always lived there. You started to play chess with the priest, taught Mirl the Hungarian style of cooking and Lois good manners. It was suddenly revealed to the men in the village that a Countess might be an amiable sort of woman, not at all high and mighty or anything. They found that she would even let you buy her a gentian brandy, when you wished to show the extreme respect in which you held her by inviting her to the White Horse. As soon as they discovered that you knew something about horses, they came running in to you one after the other, wanting you to go and see to their mares or foals. At last I had to explain to them that medical attendance on their horses must now cease, as it wasn't so much the animals they were interested in as the Countess.

"The time passed very quickly for us at that period. But after four months we began longing to see the Majestic One again. And one day we packed up and paid a visit to Vienna. We slipped into the Spanish Riding School early in the morning, pretending to be ordinary sight-seers. Luckily it had been raining, so Leopold would be training the Majestic One in the Riding Hall. We stood upstairs in the gallery and found the splendid white room, with its baroque design, as enchanting as ever. No sound could be heard but the snorting of the horses and an occasional shouted order. The hoofs sank noiselessly into the soft ground. The fascinating odor of horses so enraptured our keenly developed sense of smell that we sniffed as much as we watched. At last Leopold sent for the Majestic One. The horse went well under him and brought off a fine example of the Spanish Walk. Nevertheless, you whispered to me: 'You know, I don't like the look of him!'

"I moved my head to and fro, watching carefully to see what you meant.

"In so doing I leaned too far forward. Leopold glanced

up and recognized me. He reined in and signaled to us to come down.

"The Majestic One had not allowed himself to be brought to a standstill. He advanced to meet us with Leopold still in the saddle. You could see from the horse's expression how glad he was to find us there again.

"Leopold dismounted, saying that he was not altogether satisfied with the Majestic One. It wasn't that the horse was lazy or refractory. He was simply depressed. He seemed to be suffering from a sort of homesickness. Not for nothing was Leopold called the Professor. He didn't only ride his horses. He also always kept an eye on their moods. And in the case of the Majestic One he had come to the conclusion that we had spoiled him by the sheer intensity of our affections. The Majestic One had learned to perform the *haute école* steps and figures with mechanical accuracy. But he had now reached a point at which he could get no further without showing that he enjoyed the exercise of his skill. And melancholy prevents the development of that delight in execution which is needed in every art.

" 'You two have practically turned that animal into a human being,' said Leopold. He added to me, 'You'd better take on his further training yourself.'

"He did not mean, he explained, that he could make nothing of the Majestic One. That was certainly not the case. By keeping him for a year, so that he would perhaps forget us, he could be brought up to standard. Leopold told us, however, that he himself now had a great many horses to ride in his official capacity, a number having been again passed on to him that had been found too troublesome for others to manage. Having the Majestic One's welfare at heart, therefore, he advised us to take him back. The horse had become used to the long distances of the Puszta. But he had been obliged to live like a monk recently. He only came into contact with the outside world when he was taken out of the stables to cross the road and go in under the archway into the Riding School.

" 'Well, I noticed straight away,' you said, 'that there was something wrong with the Majestic One.'

"I was annoyed with the horse, for taking up this moody attitude and making trouble for Leopold. The latter then proposed keeping him another month, during which we could watch him at work. It might be, Leopold said, that he himself had been mistaken and that our mere presence might not after all disturb the Majestic One but actually have a good influence on him.

"At this period, accordingly, we began to spend half our days in the Spanish Riding School. We even, if you remember, made use of a special staircase which led up from the Summer Riding School to the royal box in the gallery."

The Hungarian nodded, as if she had been a grandmother indulging in romantic memories of a distant past.

"Yes, yes," she said. "I remember. It was dark there and we called it the Kissing Stair."

I nodded in my turn, like the toothless graybeard who might share such reminiscences, and murmured: "Ah, yes, those were good times! But don't let's talk of them, we shall only make ourselves miserable! The Majestic One, just then, was making us miserable enough. At the pillar exercise he behaved as though he were going to be hanged. He didn't give one decent performance of the *piaffe*, got out of step every time. Do you remember the Professor's

Neapolitano Bionda, the horse that could do all the *haute école* movements on the long rein and a *levade* as well? One or other of us always used to say, while we were watching him, that our Majestic One would never be able to do as much, because the spiritual bond between him and the Professor had weakened, for which we alone were to blame, since we had treated him as if he had been our son instead of just our horse. So one day we put him on the train again. Leopold was quite cut up about it and could not make up his mind whether he himself, rather than the horse, had not been at fault. The fact that such doubts occurred to him only showed what a great teacher he was.

"This time the Majestic One had to travel alone in his truck. How anxious we two fools were that he should arrive in good shape and have everything he needed during the few hours of the journey!

"On reaching the estate, we again placed him among the horses on the Puszta, by way of punishment, we said. But the rascal enjoyed himself so much there that it was very far from being a punishment for him. In order to make sure that he would at any rate be of some use, I rode him every day. 'We might be able to make a jumper of him, anyhow,' you remarked. And he did take the hazards well, without jibbing. We soon found how good Leopold's School in Vienna had been for the Majestic One. He was now able to jump merely by flexing his haunches. Even when he missed the right spot for taking off and came too close to the obstacle, whereupon any other horse would have re- fused, the supple joints of his hindquarters enabled him to take a sudden leap and bring me over safely——"

"Wait a bit!" the Hungarian interrupted. "When I saw you two making those jumps——"

"You said we'd have to make a *levade* champion of him——"

"Because of his strength and the flexibility of his hind-quarters!" she cried, taking the words out of my mouth.

"I say, who's doing the talking, you or I?" I asked.

"You are, of course! I only wanted to make sure you didn't fall into the error of supposing that you were the only one who realized what the Majestic One could do!" she retorted, with that special amiability of hers, which she used to make me swallow the most unpalatable home-truths.

"Well," I continued, "one day Ferencz arrived. When he saw me jumping with the Majestic One, he started taking me to task for spoiling the horse.

"'What are you talking about?' I asked him. 'A pupil that has been dismissed from the Spanish Riding School will never be any good as a trained performer!'

"Ferencz said he would like to test that statement. You backed him up and the end of it was we took the Majestic One to Budapest and I rode him there at Ferencz's establishment. On one occasion the Principal of the Budapest Spanish Riding School was looking on and you were standing next to him. After I had dismounted he immediately said that he would place his own establishment, where there were pillars, at our disposal. No horse could be properly trained without pillars, he said. I could see from the look of you that you were agreeing with the Principal and telling him the whole story of the Majestic One's failure. With you people in Hungary there's never more than a second's pause between conceiving an idea and carrying it out. We Austrians require the approval of at least three authorities first. You simply do the thing. Accordingly, the Majestic One was taken up to the royal stables at the Castle and work began in the riding ring. He allowed me to harness him to the pillars without trouble. But it took him a long time to achieve a regular beat in the pawing exercise.

"But one day, when we had almost despaired of success and I was walking away in a rage, leaving him standing between the pillars, the Principal suddenly called me back. I turned, and saw that the Majestic One had begun to perform the *piaffe* of his own accord. As soon as I started giving him the time by clicking my tongue, he really got down to it.

"The rascal had learned more from Leopold in Vienna than he had let on. It was only to prevent our losing patience with him that he had suddenly begun to perform the *piaffe*.

"He had given you and Ferencz, who had never lost faith in the Majestic One, just what you both wanted. To add to my discomfiture, Ferencz also managed one morning to persuade the Majestic One to raise his forelegs, thus executing a *pesade*. The attitude remained very stiff and the forefeet were not drawn up at all high. But I couldn't deny it was a true *pesade*, the preliminary stage of the magnificent *levade* curtsey.

"Both Ferencz and, I am sorry to say, also you yourself, Hungarian, pulled my leg unmercifully, telling me I wasn't much of a rider and offering to make me a present of a donkey."

"What nonsense! You know perfectly well that it was

only my delight with the Majestic One that made me get on your tail with Ferencz!" cried the Hungarian. She would never let it be said of her that she had ever seriously doubted my capacities, either as a man or a rider.

"After this the Majestic One must have suddenly grown tremendously keen on *haute école* work. For every day he did better and better at the Spanish Walk, while in the *piaffe* and all the other paces he regularly performed the most imposing steps. He became more and more reliable and his disposition improved continuously. At last we had only to think of something for him to do and he did it at once. Of course he was occasionally in too much of a hurry. As soon as he had mastered the switch, in a single movement, from one gallop to the other, he instantly proceeded to scorn my assistance and continued to switch in one movement out of sheer joy at being able to do so even when I tried to make him switch in three movements. But after his first excitement was over we were able to perform this exercise, too, in perfect harmony.

"At any rate the Majestic One, by the time he returned to the estate, had deserved his name to some extent, as a skilled performer as well as in other respects.

"Then we started thoroughly enjoying ourselves. One day we worked and the next we rode out early in the morning on to the Puszta and joined those herds of yours, Hungarian. They were a splendid lot now.

"But your fondest wish, Marika, still remained unfulfilled. Deflorata, employed as your carriage horse, and the Majestic One, should have been a pair. The fault was not Deflorata's. She would have been only too glad to earn her name in actual fact, but——"

"Don't try to be funny with the old tags of Latin you still haven't forgotten!" the Hungarian admonished me.

"All right then," I continued. "So Deflorata had to be a tender virgin still. She had done her level best to seduce the Majestic One. But apparently he did not yet consider himself, at six years old, ready for the joys of marriage. He seemed to regard Deflorata's caresses as mere tokens of friendship and showed no inclination to return her love. Evidently he possessed more staying power than you, Hungarian! You kept him locked up in the loose-box alone with Deflorata for three whole months. When it looked as though nothing would ever happen between those two, you went about in a kind of trance. There were often days on which you declined to see anybody, even me. You would be out with your horses on the Puszta and once more I made a mistake in supposing that I should never be able to understand you——"

"Please, Unholy George, do stop now, won't you?" begged the Hungarian, gazing at me solemnly.

"I was just going to, Marika!"

She looked so utterly forlorn that I had to take her in my arms to banish the memory of the affliction that then fell so heavily upon us. At first she had been very happy in her solitude. Her life had become an inner one, for she knew that within her something was trying to come into existence and grow, a sacred thing born of the hours in which she had given me the name of Unholy George. I had just been forced to the conclusion that she was slipping away from me when Leopold wrote to ask whether I could come to Vienna. He had a school-trained horse for me to ride in the Tournament.

The Hungarian at once told me that I ought to go. But she did not want to come with me. She added that I could also go and pay a visit to the house, to see whether Lois was looking after it properly, as after all we should be going back there in the spring. We had arranged to spend six months of every year regularly on the estate and at the house alternately. I never suspected at that time that Marika wanted to give me pleasure by bringing our child into the world at our house in the village.

So I let myself be persuaded that it was my duty to go. It was settled that I should be away three weeks but not a day longer. If I could fix everything up in a fortnight, she said, that would be fine.

She drove me to the station and laughed as she waved good-by.

When I returned a fortnight later, Janos met me at the station. He told me the Countess had not been able to come, as she was not feeling too well.

"Drive all out, Janos," I said. "So long as you don't snap the harness. Did she have an accident? Anything serious?"

Janos shook his head, muttering that it was nothing special. But I didn't believe him.

Marika was lying in the long chair on the veranda, almost all the color gone from her cheeks. She always used to look suntanned and had an extremely healthy and fresh complexion. Her face now presented a yellowish appearance. It frightened me.

"Marika, what's the matter with you?"

"Nothing, Unholy George," she answered, with a smile

that was obviously forced. "I've got to be allowed the luxury of being ill occasionally, you know!"

"And you never wrote me anything about it! There I was, out in the great world, while you——"

"Oh, nonsense! The important thing is that you were second to Leopold in the training trials tournament! I'm so proud of you!"

But I wasn't going to be side-tracked like that. As soon as Marika had gone to sleep I summoned Janos and made him swear to tell me everything, whatever the Countess might have ordered him to the contrary.

He made me swear in my turn that I would never give him away. Then he explained.

We had bought an Arab stallion, one from the Gidran stud, getting him cheap because he had developed a vile temper owing to improper treatment. We were convinced, however, that we could reform him. He was a four-year-old and we saw no reason why he should not be amenable to kindness.

The Majestic One, however, hated him. It seemed as though he were sure the Gidran horse could never be anything but a rogue at bottom. The latter did become more amiable in time. But I was always on my guard, in his neighborhood, against bites or kicks. If I ever turned my back on him, I always faced about the next moment, as I couldn't rid myself of the idea that he might attack me from behind. He had been spoiled by such handling as only human beings can give a horse and thus been made cowardly and spiteful.

Every morning while I was away, Marika drove out to inspect the herd, which included the Majestic One. It was her regular habit to alight and mingle with the horses on foot, giving each of them a slap on the neck. The Majestic One always kept jealously close to her. On one occasion she was approaching the Gidran when the Majestic One neighed shrilly. As she turned to look at him, the Gidran reared behind her and struck out. The Majestic One came bounding up in great leaps and reared to face the Gidran. Before Marika had time to move she found herself caught between the fighting stallions.

The Gidran was struck on the head by one of the Majestic One's forefeet and dropped, knocking Marika down as he fell.

Janos rushed up a moment later and dragged her clear. She had fainted. He drove her back to the estate in the carriage and instantly rode for all he was worth into Kecskemét to fetch the doctor.

The Majestic One did not leave the Gidran till the latter ceased to move. He was afterward found dead on the spot. The Majestic One had stamped the other's bones to pieces as he lay on the ground, and was splashed with his blood from head to foot.

When the doctor arrived, the Majestic One was dashing about in the courtyard, neighing wildly. He did not calm down till he was with Deflorata in the loose-box.

Janos knew nothing more. I had to apply to the doctor to hear the worst. The bruising Marika had received had caused a miscarriage. That brief and sinister statement explained everything. And the Countess, said the doctor, would never be able to have another child.

We never discussed this misfortune together. We couldn't. The one who had mentioned it would have shown lack of sympathy with the other. We thus maintained a conspiracy of silence, year after year, concerning the worst misfortune which ever happened to us. Consequently, we were able to endure it. It was a poor wretch of a horse, ruined by human beings, that had brought this sorrow upon us both. But we never made such unfortunate animals suffer for it. Heaven has bestowed more good nature and generosity upon them than upon men. Marika has become a real madonna where horses are concerned, at the cost, perhaps, of the sacrifice of what she might otherwise have come to love best.

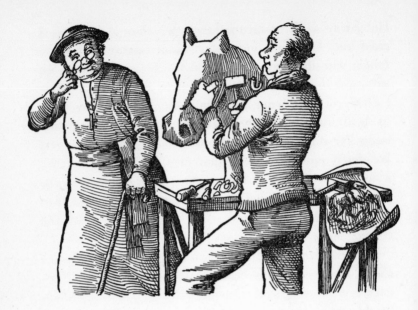

13

Lois was not satisfied with the photographs he had taken. He considered it necessary, after all, to work from the living models, the Hungarian, the Majestic One, and myself. So we sat and stood for him throughout the best hours of the day, which we could well have employed to better purpose. But it was all in a good cause. And we had led the priest such a dance recently that it was about time we did something to please him. I wondered, though, whether he would really enjoy seeing his pagans, as he called us, composing, in effigy, a sacred group. I told Lois he had better represent Saint George with his visor down, as my own features are not particularly charming. The

Hungarian said, however, that if she showed her face I must too. And Lois added that Saint George had never fought with his visor down, though Unholy George, to be sure, did so. . . .

"Oh, rot! That's not my style at all!" I snapped at him. "I've always been ready to answer, all my life, for anything I've done. Take the thing off the helmet altogether. We don't want the blasted visor!"

We were in Lois' garden. He was standing close to the Majestic One's head and trying to chisel a likeness to it in the rough wooden horse skull he had already cut to the correct shape.

As I watched the stallion crouching in the low posture of his *levade*, with his head proudly erect and the Hungarian in the saddle, I remembered an incident in which the Majestic One and I had held our own. We had been invited to a riding exhibition and . . .

"Do you remember, Hungarian," I asked, "that show when they said all a School-trained horse can do is to swagger about, and even insinuated that the Majestic One and I had been simply doing circus stunts?"

"Yes, I do," she said. "Tell Lois about it. That'll stop him pulling your leg about visors!"

"Well, my lad," I began, "our first item in that exhibition was to show the audience some classical *haute école* riding. A few Mr. Know-alls, who could only ride with their big mouths, said we were just putting up a circus turn. One actually wanted to know whether the Majestic One could jump and whether I could take him over the difficult course where steeplechasing was to take place the following day.

"They all grinned derisively as they looked at me. But the Hungarian kicked me twice under the table of the restaurant where we were sitting, as much as to say, 'Take them on!'

" 'All right,' I said quietly, 'if there's still time for me to enter, I'll be at the post with the Majestic One.'

"No one raised any objection. They proceeded, more from bumptiousness than good nature, to show me the course on the plan, pointing out its difficult hazards. I told them not to bother. I said I wouldn't even let the Majestic One see the obstacles beforehand. I'd only just look over the course myself. Some then took exception to the Majestic One, who was a ten-year-old at that time, being entered. They tried to get Leopold to dissuade me on the ground that a School-trained horse ought not to be used as a chaser. But they didn't cut any ice with Leopold. He told them it was about time proof was given of the many-sided training provided by *haute école* riding, formerly part of the art of cavalry warfare. He offered to bet that the Majestic One and I would be in the first three. Next day, when the jumping started, I watched from the stand. Meanwhile the Majestic One was being provided with a borrowed 'chaser's saddle, which was an utter misfit. The Hungarian was with him. When at last it came to our turn to ride, our starting number being the final one, not one of the competitors had covered the course without a mistake.

"Leopold was present when I mounted. He said our best chance would be to keep some time in hand, but not attempt any great speed, and to guard carefully against touching a hurdle. He gave me a nod and the Majestic One a slap on the hindquarters. The Hungarian also nodded, screwing up her eyes at me. She meant that she expected us to do our best.

"I wouldn't have risked it with any other horse. With the Majestic One I didn't have to exert myself at all, believe me! He galloped off quietly from the start. All I had to make sure of was that I didn't bother him while he was jumping. Just in front of the wall-jump I gave him a bit of a lift and he almost seemed to take offense at my attempt to prescribe what he was to do. He took the water-jump with a long and splendid leap. I did have to indicate direction, as he couldn't very well read the numbers on the obstacles, but that was absolutely all I contributed to his victory. We reached our destination in faultless fashion and in a little under the lowest time made till then, enough to insure we had won, which was all we wanted.

"The spectators cheered us to the echo. Subsequently the talk was all to our advantage. It could hardly have been anything else. They had to admit that the Majestic One had done what I said he would.

"Leopold embraced me. And as only the Majestic One's neck happened to be free at that moment, the Hungarian put her arms round his."

"Wish I'd been there," said Lois. "There'll never be another horse like the Majestic One! He can do the *haute école* stuff, jump, and even pull a cart. He doesn't think anything beneath his dignity. Our church certainly won't be able to find a better Saint George's horse. Or a more expert Saint George either!"

"And you won't be able to find a better horse-madonna, Lois!" I told him.

"I never labor the obvious," he retorted. "Good lord! Here comes the priest!"

There could be no objection, however, to the priest coming and looking on, because Lois was still only working on the horse's head. While I had been talking he had made good progress. The Majestic One's features were now clearly recognizable.

The priest was most affable. He behaved as though the affair of the book and Schwaiger's signboard had never occurred. He had forgiven and forgotten, as his profession enjoins. If he hadn't been such a patient and indulgent man, he would never have been the village priest, and our friend, for so many years.

"Well, Lois," he observed, with a laugh. "I see you're taking the Countess as a model for Saint George now!"

"She's not so heavy for the Majestic One, you see, when he's doing the *levade,* as Unholy George would be!"

The Hungarian always made the Majestic One perform the *levade* whenever Lois, for artistic reasons, required it. She now announced that the sitting was at an end. The stallion must have his sugar and she a coffee. Mirl would make it. The priest also declared he was in favor of coffee, and as Mirl, too, wanted some herself, a table was soon brought out into the garden bearing all the necessary adjuncts for the ceremony.

"Yes, it would have been a good idea, Father, for the Countess to pose for Saint George. But her build's too delicate, really. Our other friend's figure suits the part better!"

He meant me. The priest said, with a smile: "Yes, his figure's all right, I'm sure. But what about the rest of him?"

Lois, having once begun to lay careful plans for the priest's ultimate acceptance of the group, was not going to stop now.

"It's an excellent proposal, that," he said. "I mean, about the Countess."

"You could make a horse-saint of her," I suggested, to back him up.

"A madonna for horses?" exclaimed the priest. "Impossible!"

"We've got one in Hungary, all the same," said the Hungarian. "There's an image of her in the middle of the Puszta, where the horses graze. . . ."

The priest immediately wanted to know why. After all, such matters were his special province.

The Hungarian told him what had happened in that part of the country long before the war. I had heard this beautiful story from her once before. It is bound to warm the hearts of all lovers of horses and of those who love men according to whether they treat horses well or not. The Hungarian's tale went as follows:

"One evening a light carriage drove up to visit the horses on the Puszta. The reins were held by a young woman. The herdsman recognized and greeted her. She told him she wanted to stay with the horses. But he did not take her seriously and, as soon as it grew dark, rode off to the camp. The young woman sent her horse home with the carriage. It trotted away with the reins trailing. When night fell, the young woman lay down to rest among the mares that were in foal. They may have been surprised to perceive that she was weeping. It was evident to the mare nearest to her that she needed protection and warmth. The young woman was a victim of one of those common love stories with an unhappy ending. The man whom the young woman loved had already been absent, with his cavalry regiment, for half a year and she could no longer hide the evidence of how deeply she had loved him. At her home they talked of nothing else but the shame she had brought upon the family. When her time drew near, she could not bear to remain among her relatives any longer. She ran away to find refuge elsewhere and thought she would be happiest among the mares, for they, too, carried a new and growing life within them. With them she was no longer obliged to feel forsaken. Gradually peace returned to her heart. It was necessary, in fact, for her to pluck up courage and make sure of rest.

"The mare that was warming her and providing a pillow for her head began to stir. The animal, with a low, gentle neigh, raised its head. At the same moment a small hand, seeking something to hold, clutched her mane fast. The mare stayed where she was, not daring to move.

"The other mares that lay around her stood up. They sniffed, with hanging heads, at the ground where their human charge was lying.

"As the early morning twilight began to appear in the east, the young woman could discern the dark shapes of the horses and feel the warm, comforting breath of those that stood nearest her. She felt safe within the circle of mares and thanked God for their unwavering support of her.

"The herdsman on watch beside the dead embers of the campfire woke his companion as the sky reddened toward morning. 'Listen,' he said, 'wasn't that a mare neighing?'

But the other answered that no horse could utter so shrill a sound. The next moment they were swinging themselves into the saddle.

"But they could not penetrate the herd. The mares had formed a defensive circle and many lashed out at the herdsmen.

"The latter, being unable to understand the puzzling behavior of the mares, cracked their long, short-handled whips, made a breach in the ring of excited animals, and burst through it, among the whirling hoofs. They leaped from their saddles, knelt down, and removed their hats. They stared like those other herdsmen who once gazed upon a miracle both human and divine, in that stable of long ago.

"For to these two simple and kindly men a miracle had indeed happened. They were so strongly moved by it that they never dreamed of rendering assistance but continued to stare at the young woman, whom they knew, and who returned them such a faint, unearthly smile.

"Wrapped in the horse blanket that had formed a covering for the driving seat of the carriage lay a wailing child.

" 'Holy Saint Stephen!' exclaimed the two herdsmen with one voice. The young mother begged them to help her.

"One of them rode at breakneck speed to the estate to fetch a carriage. When it arrived, the horses panting wildly and the drops of sweat glistening like snowflakes on their hides, he who had been the cause of it all sprang down from the box. He had returned the night before, in the nick of time. The young family, guided by God and drawn by two good horses, drove with every precaution back to the estate. It was in a double capacity, as mother and as lady of the house, that the young woman entered it.

"The herdsmen wished to erect a visible record of the miracle. The owner of the estate had an impressive memorial shrine put up at the very spot where his child had been born among the horses. It consisted of a mosaic representing the Madonna with the Child in her arms and horses on each side of her. A substantial roof was placed in position to protect the mosaic below, where the supporting post entered the ground, stood an earthenware jar, in which the herdsmen arranged the species of Puszta grass which they call Orphan Girl's Hair, it is so fine, silky, and spotless, with its white pistils. Everyone who rode past the shrine presented his due tribute of honor and love to the Madonna of the Horses. Some, who were men, paid her a special visit to beg her to bless their herds. Mothers came to gain confidence from her in dealing with their children, always such a constant source of anxiety.

"All around the shrine grazed the mares, in foal or already delivered. In the bad times that came after the great war, when in Hungary justice and faith in God were forcibly annihilated by brutal violence, an attempt was made to drive away the herds and to destroy the image of the Madonna of the Horses. But the mares, which had long since ceased to be those of the former time, again formed a ring of defense. The rabble of thieves could not trust their own stolen mounts and so retreated. And the Madonna of the Horses now stands on the Puszta for all eternity."

A most beautiful legend, the priest observed. It really ought to be written down.

Lois said he would like to illustrate it.

Mirl simply stared into the distance and said nothing. I looked into the Hungarian's eyes. There was something she knew, but had not mentioned, in connection with that story of the Madonna of the Horses. She had not told us that the child, a girl, had been christened Marika. Only she, myself, and Janos knew that fact now, since the parents were gone. The mother had died soon after giving birth to the little Marika. And the father had been shot during the Revolution.

The priest must have been pleased with us, as we sat there, his four heathens, unwilling to talk any more in case we lost the contentment we felt in the hour that was slowly fading into early evening, while the sun went down behind the mountains, the birds ceased singing and it grew so quiet that I could hear my own heart beating and the Hungarian's too, that belonged to me. All of us, we two and our friends, were in benevolent mood. The Majestic One thrust his head between our shoulders. He skirmished with the Hungarian for a time. Then he stretched his neck out toward the table, where some sweet cakes were lying on a plate.

It made us smile and we glanced at one another. Evening was coming on and that is a time when God's most glorious creatures, horses and human beings, are wont to think of supper. Earth had us in her toils again. But the earth is a good place, for heaven is over it.

14

$\mathcal{J}$ had to practice a little fraud on the Hungarian to
prevent her insisting on our leaving for her estate at once.
My leg, in fact, was all right again now. But I still limped
with it, though I found it more difficult every day to give a
convincing performance. I wanted to stay long enough to
see the new Saint George put up in the church. But the
Hungarian considered it would be a better plan if we kept
out of the affair and didn't begrudge Lois the sole honors.
She seemed now to feel rather sorry she had permitted herself to be immortalized with us in that magnificent wooden
group. Lois was just then putting the finishing brush strokes
to it, to give the whole thing an agreeably gay appearance,

such as the taste of the people here for bright colors would enjoy. She therefore wished to leave as soon as my ankle had healed. I was to accompany her in the Gentian and the Majestic One would just have to go by train.

"It's too early yet, Hungarian!" I exclaimed. As a rule we did not leave for her place till autumn was approaching. "And what about my leg? I can feel every change of the weather in it!"

The weather, however, let me down. So nowadays I only make very vague predictions. On that occasion I said that my ankle was twitching and that we should therefore be having some rain, whereupon eight days passed without our ever catching sight of a single rain cloud, even the tiniest. Luckily, however, we heard some thunder, so the Hungarian was nevertheless obliged to admit that my leg could be relied on to some extent.

Unfortunately Lois turned up just then and asked whether I would like to go with him to the skittle party at the "Ox," where the villagers, he said, were already having a high old time of it. Hadn't we heard the clatter? Since that day my bad leg had done me no good at all. Soon afterward the Hungarian advised me not to forget to limp when I thought she wasn't looking. Then she revived the subject of the *capriole*, which we still hadn't performed. As there was no help for it, I did my best with the Majestic One. But we didn't succeed. The Hungarian's silence on this occasion spoke volumes. By the evening I couldn't stand it any longer and said the *capriole* story had been a vile falsehood. The horse dung, I said, had been the true cause of the accident, but I had considered it too utterly shameful for a horseman to have experienced so unseemly a misfortune. I had to give a precise account of the whole incident. At first the Hungarian laughed. Then she said, in a most reproachful tone, "Aren't you ashamed of yourself, Unholy George? Fancy telling such a lie!"

"Yes, indeed," I answered. "I really do regret it most deeply."

"I should always come, let me tell you, whether you simply fell off your horse or into the dung off your own feet," the Hungarian retorted, in maternal wrath. "Have you any more frauds to confess? You'd better speak out, while we're on the subject!"

"No, I really can't think of anything else at the moment," I rejoined.

"Well, when you do, just tell me, will you? Perhaps it was you, actually, who ate up my rock garden? Can you swear it was the Majestic One?"

"Yes, I really can, Hungarian," I declared with emphasis. "Surely you know I don't believe in vegetarianism. I'm much more carnally minded, like the villagers, whom the priest is always lecturing for eating too much!"

As soon as I spoke of being carnally minded the Hungarian's eyes flashed with anger. She hates my making that sort of joke. I therefore at once changed the subject.

"Oh, by Jove, yes, Hungarian!" I exclaimed all of a sudden. "I do remember something now. But it wasn't a lie. It was more like embezzlement, really."

"Good heavens, Unholy George! How much did you——"

"Oh no, there wasn't any money involved. Only a letter."

"Hand it over at once, please!"

"But I haven't got it. It was a letter I was going to write. To you!"

"Well, well!" commented the Hungarian, in a tone of curiosity. "And what did you intend to put in it?"

"I was going to say the Majestic One had gone sick. It was when we had arranged to leave in March and you stayed on because you wanted to sell those cattle . . ."

"Yes, go on!"

"I am going on!"

"You keep beating about the bush!"

"Well, I found when I got home that the Majestic One had caught the strangles. His nose and mouth were running continuously and within a week he had begun to lose weight so fast that I could foresee the exact time when he would be gone altogether! Every day I told myself that I ought to write to you. But I kept thinking that the trouble would soon be over and in the end he did get better. I only wanted to spare you anxiety, Hungarian."

"You've given me quite a scare! Even though it was a retrospective one. Suppose anything actually had happened! You'll never do that again, Unholy George, will you?"

"Well, it's all over and done with now, Hungarian."

"That's what you think! Just feel how my heart's beating!"

When I obeyed and stroked the place to make the heart underneath return to normal, my hand was slapped.

"That's not where my heart is," she said. "Keep your fingers under control, will you? And anyhow, look here, what about getting on with the story?"

"Oh, the story's finished now. Shall I tell you how the

wedding of the Majestic One and Deflorata eventually came about? You were there yourself when he suddenly realized he was a stallion and started——"

"I think you'd better cut that part," the Hungarian broke in, talking so fast that I wasn't able to utter another word. "You're such a simpleton that you're quite likely to go into unnecessary details. And I'm perfectly well aware what happens when a stallion makes love to a mare!"

"I was going to put it quite nicely, Hungarian, about the Majestic One neighing as we had never heard him neigh before, just previous to——"

"That'll do, that'll do, Unholy George! I don't want to go cold all over between one word and the next, for fear you're going to come out with something awful, after which you'll just gulp and mumble that that's the way it is with horses and pull a face like a sick saint. Your wall mottoes will be quite enough to go on with for the present!"

"All right then, let's talk about the foal, the Majestic One's son, and how he started breeding our own Lipizzaners, after I had bought a Favory stallion at the Bábolna auction and you had got hold of some fillies from the Esterhazy stud——"

"I don't believe we've any more strictly historical material left, Unholy George," she said.

"Oh, but we have," I answered. "You've forgotten the Majestic One's great day, haven't you? The day when he proved, in the Spanish Riding School in Vienna, that he amounted to something after all?"

"Oh yes, that's right," she said. "He did his best *levades* there and Leopold was very pleased with him. And then they made a porcelain statuette of the Majestic One in

Augarten. He became quite a famous horse and nowadays we really ought to be grateful to him for allowing us to go on riding him!"

"The mere fact that we came to own him was a bit of luck for us, Hungarian," I observed. "If the Majestic One had never existed, our own story would never have existed either!"

"And what an awful thing it would have been if we two had not found each other," said the Hungarian.

I gave her a sharp look. For I wasn't sure whether she was speaking in jest or earnest.

She gazed back at me, saying, "I don't think I should want to live, if it were not for horses—and you!"

The Hungarian made her declaration of love with such simplicity that I could only answer her with my eyes, thinking what a good thing it was our lives were so arranged that we were always meeting each other afresh. We alternately parted and reunited several times a year, so that custom could never stale the hours we spent together, and spoil our love.

"I say, we ought to give the Majestic One another lump of sugar," Marika suggested. She must have guessed my thoughts. "He's been so good while he's been traveling around with us horse gypsies!"

We walked over to the stable. The Majestic One had already lain down. He began to get up when he saw us.

But the Hungarian slapped his neck and gave him the sugar before he could rise. He lay there chewing and watching us. I had my arm round the Hungarian. He had seen us in that posture often enough. But now he pricked up his ears. His low neighing sounded just as though he understood and enjoyed our happiness.

"Yes, yes! In another two weeks you'll be with her, that Deflorata of yours!" the Hungarian told him.

"In two weeks?" I repeated.

"Well, that's about the time it will take for the new Saint George group to be put up in the church," she answered.

"I thought you wanted to leave before then?"

"Well, if you two are not coming I can wait a bit longer just for that reason."

"That's very good of you, Hungarian," I said. "I shan't have to hop round like an invalid any more, then!"

"There now!" she exclaimed. "I felt sure at the time, when you were confessing, that you were keeping another of your tricks dark!"

I yawned elaborately, observing, "Good lord, how sleepy I am!"

The Hungarian smiled at me, shaking her head over her own shortcomings.

"I've known you such a long time now! But I fall for those same old tricks you play me, every time! Well, let's go, then. I shall be quite interested to see whether you're really sleepy or——"

"Or what?"

"Or just wishful."

15

A book like this must come to an end some time. But life goes on, it seems, and leaves what we call the conclusion behind. Sitting over this last chapter, however, and turning back a few pages to look at what has already been committed to paper, I feel I ought to have said a lot more. Then I find, on reflection, that there's too much of it, all jumbled up together, with absolutely no artistic control. Art demands strict proportion and clear lines. It needs those very rules, in fact, which have to be observed by riders of the *haute école*.

But reins are as easy for me to hold as a pencil is difficult. The tip of the middle finger of my right hand has already developed a corn. In this chair, too, I could never keep the firm seat the Majestic One knows so well when I ride him. And I always stopped writing when I heard him moving about outside. It regularly gave me quite a lot of trouble to pick up the thread of the story again where I had dropped it. As a rule, on those occasions, I began writing about something else. I'm quite sure I ought to have stuck to riding. But still I can't help thinking now it would be a pity for all that nice paper to have been scribbled over in vain. So I had better knock the thing into shape and round it off properly, just as the Majestic One and I, at the end of the morning's ride, perform an elegant *levade*. I doubt, however, whether my last chapter is likely to prove such a success as a *levade* by the Majestic One. I won't renounce the attempt, though. It may turn out all right. "A blind hen will always find her cock," is one of Lois' favorite sayings.

There isn't really much more to tell. You know us all well by now. At most you only need to hear how we, the Majestic One and I, earn our living. To begin with we eat what grows on our two fields and the grazing ground. The Majestic One eats the grass as soon as it is green and sometimes he eats the oats as well. But I myself have to take my wheat to the miller to exchange for flour. As for ready cash, we two, to use business jargon, are shareholders in the Hungarian's stud. It is true that the Majestic One does more than I do to improve the breed. But he can't very well eat the dividends, so I administer them. In more precise terms, we spend the lot or buy more horses with it.

The Hungarian and I don't really get anywhere, but we keep alive and have plenty of horses. So we're content.

Then, of course, my having my house here and the Hungarian her estate on the Puszta, which makes us travel a good deal, so that the Majestic One is quite well known on the railway, may surprise some people who haven't yet stopped being surprised at us. Well, you see, the Hungarian is very fond of her home and so am I of mine, but each of us is also fond of the other one's place, so neither of us has yet suggested that we should set up house together. I only mention this fact at all because otherwise you might think we had a screw loose. We only leave one home to go to another and we're always with horses that know us quite well, because we have been looking after them ever since they left the womb and became foals with long, stiff legs. Now that I can see it all so clearly as I look back I am sure that horses, in our case, have played the part of destiny. They have brought us both joy and sorrow. It would certainly have gone worse with us, though, if human beings had taken a hand in the game. Everything that happened to us had some significance, even the horse dung that got in my way. It's true that when we come among strangers we have to leave our riding breeches behind, patched again and again as they are and worn through at the patches owing to our ruling passion, and we always feel that there is something missing when we put on ordinary clothes. The Hungarian says it's that good, healthy smell of horses and she's probably perfectly right. Our reaction to cities is just the same as that of horses. We soon get tired of walking on pavements. We have quite a soft spot for Salzburg and Vienna, and in Hungary, the cities are always given a rural aspect by the peasants' carts that come in, drawn by those deer-necked horses of theirs. But elsewhere we regularly see to it that we have good hoofs under us. I'm glad we're now off again to the Puszta, where the plain never ends. How we ride, once we get there!

Saddle and harness creak, the rhythmic hoofbeats make a muffled sound, the horses snort. Sometimes, when there was a storm brewing, we used to race it home. When we dismounted in the courtyard under the first drops of rain, we would slap the necks of our gallant steeds. Nikolaus Lenau, who was a Hungarian, with the same tastes as ourselves, horseman as well as poet, wrote such a glorious set of verses on this theme that I know it by heart.

> *Tumultuous the storm clouds race*
> *Like horses through the sky*
> *And at a thundered gallop's pace*
> *The echoing hunt goes by.*
>
> *The tempest is a plainsman bold*
> *Bawling a lusty song,*
> *The lightning's whip he doth unfold*
> *To drive his herds along.*
>
> *But soon the horses run with sweat,*
> *Their hoofbeats faint must grow,*
> *Till the hot and heavy raindrops wet*
> *The long heathland below.*

The Hungarian doesn't care much for thundering cloud-horses, though in other respects she has enough courage for two men. Once, when we were helping the herdsmen, during a storm, to get the panic-stricken animals home, she had seen a mare struck by lightning. Her own horse reared up in a fright and went over backward. I had to pull Marika out from under the poor beast. Its back was broken. She herself had two ribs smashed and after they had been set again all she suffered from as a result was a fear of storms. Consequently we got into the habit of running races with rain clouds and so far our gallant steeds have always given us the victory.

The course of true love does not always run smooth. But the more trouble our horses involuntarily got us into the more constant our love became. I sometimes wonder whether the Hungarian is so fond of me for the very reason that I give her pain. During the last few days she's been singing her beautiful old Hungarian folk songs quite a lot. They have so sweet and sad a sound that I always fall for them and begin longing for my other, Hungarian, home. All I know of her language, apart from a few common turns of speech, are the words of those songs. One word of her language I like better than all the rest when she speaks it. She pronounces it in a great variety of tones. It is *igén*, which means yes. *Nem*, which is Hungarian for no, she never uses in reply to me, perhaps because my wishes invariably coincide with her own. It may also be that love can never say no, even when it is terribly hard to say yes.

The Majestic One, too, will certainly be glad to get away. He knows we don't work so hard at *haute école* on the estate but prefer to go galloping far and wide over the grassy plain. So those visits are real horse-holidays for him. On the riding ground behind the house, however, all paces must be seriously studied, to make the result a genuine work of art, a silent music of movement producing a fleeting image which cannot be caught and arrested like a picture or a poem. It has to be renewed every day, because it is a living thing, controlled by the laws of life itself. One day it will come to an end altogether, for a horse's life does not last as long as we should like it to. But I don't care to think of that. We have never mentioned to each other the possibility that in fifteen years' time we may not have a Majestic One any more.

Leopold has sometimes told us about the horses he has lost. At such times he lowers his voice, so as to avoid recalling such painful memories too clearly to mind.

The Majestic One's sons and daughters possess his traits of nobility. But whether they will be able to console us one of these days, when our horse of destiny is no more, who can say? It may be that then I shall never get into the saddle again and that Marika and I will then have to draw still closer to each other, to keep ourselves warm. We only wish we could give our Majestic One enough years from our own lives to insure that we all finish the course at the same time.

Love of horses brings suffering, you see. But it may be that God gives them a shorter life on earth because they deserve heaven more than we do.

I can hear him again now outside. The Hungarian is leading him out of his box and harnessing him to the open cart which he pulled last year in the procession, carrying the former Saint George.

Today he is to take the new one to the church and the Hungarian is going to decorate his harness with flowers and ribbons. She has already been polishing our riding boots till we can see our faces in them. For we are going to honor Saint George today in the guise which he would probably most have wished us to assume, that of riders.

But before we reached the stage of permission being granted for the new Saint George to move in, a stiff encounter with the priest took place.

Lois had summoned us two to support him when the priest arrived to inspect the group. Our Saint George had been set up in the garden. We intercepted the priest at the garden gate, to insure that he first saw the work at a distance.

Saint George's horse glittered snow-white in the sunshine. The saint's armor had a silver sheen and a blue plume waved from his helmet. The woman he held upon his saddle bow was clothed in scarlet. Her robe streamed over the horse's white shoulder and partially covered the vigorously raised forelegs. The dragon's color was poison-green. He was spitting fire and red blood was gushing from his death-wound, in which the lance was fixed.

"Marvelous!" cried the priest, the moment he saw the colors flashing in the sun. He walked up to make a closer inspection, rather faster than we quite liked. We remained rooted to the spot, like children after doing something naughty.

The priest made a prolonged examination of the group. Then he turned round, waved to us to approach, and began his speech in quite a pacific tone of voice.

"I stick to what I said at first, Lois, that it's marvelous! Personally, I've no fault to find with it as a work of art. You know perfectly well what I do feel! But you just stand there and don't . . . I tell you, the thing's quite impossible! There'll be a lot of talk and it'll get as far as Salzburg.

Someone will come and ask what I mean by it and what am I going to say then, eh?"

"Don't you say anything, Father," Lois advised him. "In your place I should simply ask them what the hell it had to do with them!"

"But don't you see," cried the priest, "that they'll start hinting that I'm a freethinker? And they'll consider that woman an offense to morals!"

"I only made her as beautiful as the Countess herself is in life," retorted Lois impenitently.

But the priest was already speaking of the saintly rider himself. He said he considered it a downright wicked farce to take a man called Unholy George as the model for a genuine saint.

"If you're going on to say anything against the horse, I'll simply put a match to the whole thing and let it burn up and be done with!" Lois exclaimed, in quite a passion.

"You will merely complete the tale of your sins if you do," returned the priest.

Lois, red in the face with anger, said that so far as he was concerned the priest and the entire clergy could go and hang themselves. "Praise the Lord!" he added, by way of mitigation of this remark.

The priest, in his astonishment and probably also from mere habit, immediately responded with the usual "Amen!"

The Hungarian signed to me with her eyes to go and join Lois, who was already strutting off, like a stork, into the house.

"Hell's bells!" he growled. "Mirl, get me a short one!"

"Me, too, please," I said. "I believe the Hungarian, with God's help, will be able to convince the priest."

Lois grunted.

"She may be able to tame wild horses," he said, "but she'll never be able to make that priest see reason!"

"I have my doubts about the priest, but not about the Hungarian," I rejoined. Mirl said I was right.

"I'm more likely to marry Mirl," Lois muttered, "than he is to stop being pigheaded!"

Mirl smiled. Her expression seemed to indicate that the utter impossibility he mentioned was quite in the cards.

And when I came to look Mirl up and down, I suddenly realized what she was smiling about.

"I'll go and see how they're getting on," I observed, and went out. The priest and the Hungarian were now talking quite calmly to each other. But he was still shaking his head too often.

"I say, Father, I've got something to tell you," I began. "Lois was saying just now, in the rage he was in, that he was more likely to marry Mirl than you were to give way."

In saying this I was dangling a hook for the priest himself, who had been offering bait for such a time now to Lois and Mirl, to lure them into marriage. And the priest, telling himself, no doubt, that something was better than nothing, replied that he would accordingly impose that condition upon his assent. He would also insist, he added that the villagers should inspect the group before it was accepted and declare themselves jointly responsible for its reception into the church. Thirdly, he continued, he would like to know whether we, too, would not also be prepared to marry forthwith.

Marika had no suitable reply ready. She didn't want to

annoy the priest by giving the obvious one and also she wanted me to have my say.

"Leave us out of it, Father! Lois and Mirl have a good reason for marrying and we——"

"It's pure selfishness then," the priest lamented. "All he wants to do is is to get that group of his into the church!"

I refrained from telling him he was wrong.

But he really longed, he added, to see Marika and myself enter the holy state of matrimony.

"Please, Hungarian," I said, "do go and tell Lois that the group will be accepted for the church."

The priest looked at me in amazement, as I thus decided matters without consulting him. I buttonholed him.

"Look here, Father, those two have a good reason for marrying. Mirl is going to have a child. But the Hungarian and I can no longer expect any such thing!"

"Don't talk in that impious way!" the priest rebuked me. So I told him what had happened and how it had all come to nothing.

He held his tongue then. And when I asked him whether he would still insist in these circumstances, he simply shook his head, took my arm, and propelled me into the house.

The Hungarian had by that time somewhat appeased Lois' wrath and the priest felt it his duty to make a speech. He said the Countess had reminded him that in former days the old masters had actually painted their wives as madonnas. He then plunged into technicalities for a while and finally declared with considerable emotion that the main reason he now gave the proposal his blessing was that Lois had at long last decided to marry Mirl.

At this point Lois could contain himself no longer.

"You're all wrong there, Father," he burst out. "I should have married Mirl in any case, as soon as I found that at last we two were going to amount to something!"

But the priest still had his trump to play, the condition that the villagers were to look the group over first.

The step was taken the same day. The villagers were so bowled over by the magnificence of Saint George's horse that they didn't look at anything else whatever and declared they would have that saint or none at all.

So the new saint was ceremoniously conducted to the church, where the priest preached a sermon so crammed with analogies between the lives of horses and human beings that it was a pleasure to listen to him.

When he had finished, one of the congregation, in his enthusiasm, let out a real shout of "Bravo!" It was myself.

It was only on that evening, however, when we were all sitting together at my place, that the priest for the first time clearly proved himself to be as well shod with horse-science as a horse with good iron.

Mirl had asked what exactly the Lipizzaner breed, to which the Majestic One belonged, really was.

The priest then explained that the ancient Greeks had possessed stud farms, sacred to the gods, not far from their own country, in the rocky alpine region where the Italians still breed horses today, at Lipizza near Trieste. The Lipizzaner stud had been founded in the year 1580 by the Archduke Charles, son of the Emperor Ferdinand I. He caused horses to be brought from Spain, from Castile and Andalusia. These became the ancestors of the present Lipizzaners, which still retain today the proud, high-stepping action of their forefathers. Lipizzaners remained the property of the emperors until the Danube monarchy collapsed during the World War and Lipizza passed into the possession of Italy. Some of the horses were then taken to Piber in Styria, where our oldest bloodstock is still kept. Lipizzaners are also to be found today in Hungary, Yugoslavia, and Romania. But it is in Vienna and Budapest that the Spanish Riding Schools are situated which test the stallions to determine whether they will be suitable sires for the continuation of the breed.

"Next time you go to Vienna, Mirl," I said, "take a look at Prince Eugene in Heroes' Square. He is mounted on a Lipizzaner. The field marshals, too, of the Maria Theresa monument, are all riding Lipizzaners. But the finest of them all, really, is Prince Eugene's."

"And the best place to see what the old Spanish horses looked like," added the Hungarian, "is Salzburg, where you can see them in the Horse-Trough frescoes."

"And do you know, Mirl," I asked, "why Prince Eugene's stallion is performing a *levade*? In the old days of swordplay and pistol shots, you see, High School Riding was practiced in Naples as training for war."

I explained that a horse performing the *levade* would be shielding its rider, with its own body, from the bullets of the enemy. In the *capriole* it would be lashing out at a pursuer. At that period horses participated valiantly in the battles fought. But later on riding at the School was practiced as an art and became the best method of training both horse and rider. The Spanish Riding School in Vienna was inaugurated in 1735, with a great display of horsemanship, after its magnificent building had been erected by the young Fischer von Erlach. And today the Spanish Riding School still pursues its lofty purpose as in former times. The Majestic One's great qualities, I said, are due to the classical methods of the High School, which give horses a healthy physique, supple shoulders, and good lungs.

The Hungarian smiled at the fiery zeal with which we explained it all to Mirl, each of us trying to show we knew a little more horse-science than the others.

"Just you go into the Spanish Riding School in Vienna," she told Mirl, "and watch them at it. You'll know more then than if you listen to the men talking about horsemanship the whole evening!"

The Hungarian meant to issue a warning, intended for me. Once I start talking about horses I never stop. That's the way of it whenever Leopold and I meet. We should tell stories about Lipizzaners for days on end if it weren't for the fact that at nights we have to sleep and hold our tongues.

Marika told the priest, Mirl, and Lois that they must really come and pay us a visit in Hungary one day. The two latter agreed with enthusiasm but the priest said he couldn't leave his flock in the village for even a few days. Everything would be at sixes and sevens if he did. Sooner or later Farmer Schwaiger would remember the trick played on him with the sign board and would start roughhousing it with everyone in the village, announcing that he would be certain to have his revenge on the guilty party if he gave them all a good thrashing. No, said the priest, much as he would desire to pay his respects to the Countess, he could not neglect his duties, especially at the present time, when so dubious a representation of the new Saint George required had just been provided.

"Oh, he's not so bad as all that, Father!" exclaimed the Hungarian in my defense. For the very reason, she added, that Saint George's horse now had an expert rider, with a woman to keep a strict eye on him, the priest might feel himself at liberty to travel to Hungary, where the wine grew that he was so fond of.

The Hungarian fetched out our last bottles and the priest never failed to drink to our toasts. Wouldn't he like to hear, she inquired further, those beautiful songs they sang in the evenings on the Puszta? To give him a taste for them, she sang an old Hungarian riding song. After she had finished everyone said it was very fine, but what would the words be in German?

She did not answer, but pointed to the open window. The Majestic One, as usual, had been going his rounds through the yard and garden before lying down to sleep. He was now standing at the window and looking in, attracted by the familiar tune he had often heard us two singing on our rides. He had cocked up his ears intently, for he loved good music.

In the silence the Majestic One's proud, stallion's neigh rang out. The Hungarian slipped her left hand gently into my right, as it lay near my glass on the table. I crooked my fingers round hers and we sat thus linked, with a silent prayer in our hearts for God to grant a long and happy future for the Majestic One, for ourselves, and for you too, who love, as we do, horses of a noble breed!